D1546393

CENTURIA

By the same author

All the Errors

CENTURIA

One Hundred Ouroboric Novels

GIORGIO
MANGANELLI

Translated from the Italian by
HENRY MARTIN

McPherson & Company
KINGSTON, NEW YORK

CENTURIA

Published by McPherson & Company,
Post Office Box 1126, Kingston, New York 12402,
with assistance from the Literature Program
of the New York State Council on the Arts.
Typeset in Bodoni and Poster Bodoni.
Designed by Bruce R. McPherson.
Manufactured in the United States.
First Edition.
1 3 5 7 9 10 8 6 4 2   2005 2006 2007

Library of Congress Cataloging-in-Publication Data

Manganelli, Giorgio.
[Centuria. English]
One hundred ouroboric novels / Giorgio Manganelli ;
translated from the Italian by Henry Martin.
p.   cm.   .
ISBN 0-929701-72-0 (alk. paper)
I. Martin, Henry, 1942-   II. Title.
PQ4873.A48C4613 2004
858'.91409--dc22
20040189152

Translator's Preface

*G*iorgio Manganelli was also a kind of time machine. He was not entirely at home in the twentieth century, and looked beyond it in both directions. Or as Italo Calvino remarked in his introduction to the French edition of *Centuria*,[1] he was "the most Italian of Italy's contemporary writers, and as well the most isolated." He was the most traditional and the most *sui generis*. As remote as a classical bestiary and as close as last night's nightmare. The oxymoron was something more for Giorgio Manganelli than a favorite literary figure. His sense of the relativity of time, or even of its fragility, is also to be found in the "sources" for this book. On the one hand, one can hardly overlook the *Decameron*, and before it the hundred tales of the anonymous twelfth-century *Novellino*, for which Manganelli was asked in 1975 to supply an introduction, when it was republished by Rizzoli. *Centuria* was written in 1979. But commentators also note that Manganelli was asked by a magazine in 1978 to be a member of a jury whose task was to formulate a list of a hundred books that would "teach the public to read," and that earlier, in 1960, for another periodical, he had worked with two other writers on a project that hinged on résumés of each of "a hundred books for every household." Manganelli looked back on these experiences with a certain sense of dismay. He himself sites his inspiration for *Centuria* in the sheerest of circumstantialities: "By chance I had a number of sheets of typing paper which were slightly larger than normal, and I found myself intrigued by the thought of writing a series of narratives which each would never exceed the length of a single page: it's like the myth of the sonnet, or of a rigid and restrictive canon to which the writer must necessarly adhere."[2] And again, "I have the feeling that *Centuria*'s little stories are a bit like novels from which all the air has been removed. And that might be my definition of a novel: forty lines plus two cubic meters of air. I've settled for simply the forty lines: they take up less space. And with books, of course, you know that space is always an enormous problem." Readers will also discover *Centuria* to contain a catalogue of sins, and a modest list of virtues: one of the virtues that discreetly reappears from time to time is reticence, whereas one of the major sins is a wagging tongue.

---

1. Published in 1985, by Editions "W," in the translation of J.-B. Para.
2. In an interview with Stefano Giovanardi, published in *Avanti!*, April 8, 1979.

Author's Preface

T*he small volume now* before you holds within a brief space a vast and pleasant library; it in fact contains one hundred *romans fleuves*, but crafted in such anamorphic ways as to seem to the hasty reader to be texts of few, spare lines. It aspires, therefore, to be a prodigy of the contemporary science allied to rhetoric, recently brought to light by the local Universities. In short, a thin but endless volume; in the reading of which the readers will need to exercise the skills they already know, and perhaps to learn a few more: games with light that allow a reading between the lines, beneath the lines, between the two faces of a page, discovering the retreats of elegantly awkward chapters, of pages of noble ruthlessness, and sober exhibitionism, where they have mercifully been hidden away from children and the aged. On closer scrutiny, the considerate reader will here discover everything required for a lifetime of bookbound readings: minute descriptions of houses in Georgia where sisters destined to turn into rivals pass an adolescence at first oblivious, then turbid; sexual, passionate, carnal equivocations, minutely dialogued; memorable conversions of tormented souls; virile farewells, female constancy, inflations, plebeian tumult; gleaming appearances of heroes with a mild and terrible smile; persecutions, escapes, and behind a word I will not speak, the oblique outline of a round table on the Rights of Man.

If I am allowed to offer a suggestion, there is an optimum way to read this little book, but costly: acquire the right to the use of a skyscraper with the same number of floors as the number of the lines of the text to be read; at each floor, station a reader holding the book; assign each reader a line; on a signal, the Supreme Reader will begin to plunge from the building's summit, and as he transits progressively past the windows, each floor's reader will read the line assigned, in a loud, clear voice. It is understood that the number of the building's floors must exactly correspond to the number of the lines, and that there be no ambiguity on second floor and mezzanine, which might cause an embarrassing silence before the impact. It is also good to read it in the outer shadows, better if at absolute zero, in a capsule lost in space.

Giorgio Manganelli's "author's preface" was first published as the book jacket "advertisement" for the original Italian edition, issued by Rizzoli, as well as for subsequent Adelphi editions.

CENTURIA

ONE

Let's suppose that a person who is writing a letter to another person—their sex or sexes are immaterial—should at some point hold the suspicion, or simply perhaps have the realization, of being slightly drunk. No, it's not a question of drunk and disorderly, noisy and repugnant—if not for the fact that drunkenness is an hyperbole of existence, and as such (as we learned to write in essays) points out its intrinsic repellency.

The writer, disturbed by the revelation of his drunkenness, might simply lay down his pen. The turbid lucidity of intoxication might make it appear appropriate to abstain from further communication. But abstention from further writing would amount to having made a reasonable assessment of the forms of unreasonable behavior which typify inebriation; so, he could abdicate his writer's throne only insofar as he could identify himself as non-inebriated, and a mask, performance and counterfeit of himself while drunk. But in the moment in which he realizes, or believes himself to have grown aware of the realization of his inebriation, he has also spurned all intention or desire to give it up, nor would he tolerate doing so. So, from this moment on, his drunkenness will be voluntary, which is not an unavoidable option, even if strongly counseled by drowsiness, by moral irritation, by a bizarre admixture of discomfort and contentment, which all together he evaluates as symptoms of inebriation. So, he will continue to write. But shall he write in a particularly guarded fashion, or, quite the opposite, in an innocent, imprecise, prelapsarian way? He refuses to superintend himself, since he knows, and has always known, that caution courts silence, and that rather than the silence of abstention, it is the crude and brutal abstention of the gag. He finds innocence, however, to be equally repugnant, especially this innocence scraped together with the complicity of a glass of fermented fruit juice. Yet no sooner than he finishes writing these words, or thinking them, he cannot refrain from asking himself what other kind of innocence there might be, outside this slightly toxic fuzzy-mindedness. It's upon innocence, then, that he has to pass judgment, upon his own innocence. But is there finally no possible compromise between the cowardice of such an innocence and the dignity of a lie? "My friend," he writes, "if shame is the only thing that is not shameful, am I not, perhaps, to aspire to its innocent inner peace?" But the words contain a challenge, and enrage him.

TWO

A man of adequate education and decorous deportment made a visit, after months of absence, occasioned by horrid events of war, to the woman he loved. He did not kiss her; instead, stepping off silently into a corner, he vomited at length. He gave the astonished woman no explanation for his vomit, nor did he ever explain it to anyone else. He too had to bide his time before being able to understand that with his vomit he had also expelled from his body all the innumerable, deposited images of the woman he loved; they had made places for themselves in his body, and lovingly had filled it with toxins. But the moment in which he understood this also made it clear to him that he would no longer find it possible to treat this woman as though only love had taken place between them, a pliant love, anxious only to subdue all obstacles and to touch the other's skin, forever. He had experienced the toxicity of love, and had understood that the toxins produced by distance were only an equivalent alternative to those produced by nearness, and that he had vomited the past in order to be able to vomit the future. Though he would have found it impossible to explain, to anyone, he knew vomit rather than sighs to be the symptom of all necessary love, as death is the only certain symptom of life.

From that moment on, he has found himself with the delicious afflictions of a situation in which he is able neither to spurn, nor court, nor caress, nor contemplate the woman whom, without doubt, he loves—whom indeed he loves unbearably, now that he has made her a witness to his vomit—nor is he able to reveal his secret to her: that, in order completely to accept her, he must absorb her, make her a part of himself, to the point of her finally revealing herself as a poison, which is something she does not know herself to be, and which he does not desire to explain to her. Meanwhile, on all fronts, life grows unstable, new wars threaten. The prospective dead apparel themselves, and the soil grows soft, in expectation of graves. Posters explaining the spilling of blood are being pasted up. Everywhere. Since none of them speaks of vomit, the lover concludes that the problem is either unknown, or taken for unknown, or too well known. He kisses his fiancée, entrusts her with the nuptial night, and vomits as he takes his mount on the muscular horse of death.

THREE

An extremely meticulous gentleman has arranged for the following afternoon to meet with three people: first with the woman he loves; next with a woman he'd be able to love; lastly with a friend to whom, in short, he owes his life and perhaps his sanity. None of these persons, moreover, would play a part in his life if the others weren't likewise part of it; so the bases of the afternoon appointment, in addition to psychological, have also to do with fate. And all the same, these three persons, reciprocally necessary, are reciprocally incompatible. Neither of the women feels any affection for the friend, since neither of the women has saved the gentleman's life and sanity; indeed, their intolerant and skittish behavior had furnished the premise for the intervention of a prudent and absent-mindedly subtle friend. The friend regards the gentleman as his masterpiece, and would prefer that he not be easily accessible. The woman the gentleman loves mistrusts the woman he'd be able to love, though not so much in the light of the love that, one presumes, she consecrates to the gentleman who indeed loves her: her mistrust derives much more from the equanimity which the gentleman achieved by risking madness and finding salvation at the hands of a friend whom all would like to meet—and concerning whose savior status all have been informed—even if no one goes so far as to ask for a formal introduction. Finally, the woman the gentleman would be able to love does not return that love—a love, moreover, strictly speaking, which the gentleman has not given her—but nonetheless perceives herself as an object of potential love. And she enjoys this possibility—most likely destined to remain without development—since she sees it as the perfect mix of unconcern and passion, albeit a mix imperiled by the reality of the woman whom the gentleman truly loves, despite the fact that she herself, the woman potentially loved, could not remain in place without her, since the friend, whom she does not know, but whom she fears, perceiving him as strong and indifferent, would keep her at a distance. The gentleman has summoned these three persons and arranged for them to meet since he would like to explain and to find it demonstrated that without them his life would be impossible. He is weak and intensely mortal, and his survival depends entirely on an interplay of accidents. So, does he want to perform a scene of melodramatic confession? Never again. At this point he knows that he will not keep that appointment, since tomorrow is too narrow a space for both himself and the others' explanations. He himself, moreover, is the narrowest fact of all, and the simultaneous appearance of these three incompatible and necessary images would instantly destroy him.

FOUR

*T*oward ten o'clock in the
morning, a man of sound education and moderately
melancholy spirits had discovered an irrefutable
proof of the existence of God. It was a complex
proof, but still not so much so as to lie beyond the
grasp of a medially philosophic mind. The man of
sound education remained composed, re-examined
the proof of the existence of God from end to beginning, from left to right, from beginning to end, and
concluded he had done a good job. He closed the pad
that contained his working notes for the definitive
proof of the existence of God, and went out for no
particular reason, or, in short, to live. At about four
in the afternoon, while making his way back home,
he realized that he had forgotten the exact formulation of a few of the passages of the demonstration;
and all the passages, naturally, were essential.

It made him nervous. He entered a bar and
ordered a beer, and felt for a moment that his calm
was beginning to return. He recovered a passage, but
then immediately realized he had lost two others. He
placed his hopes in his notes, but knew his notes to
be incomplete, having left them in that condition
since he didn't want anyone, perhaps the cleaning
woman, to be certain of the existence of God before
he had meticulously articulated the whole of the argumentation. At two-thirds of the way toward home,
he realized that as the proof of the existence of God

was losing its firm, remarkable outlines, it was also spawning themes that left him uncertain as to whether or not they in fact had belonged to his original argumentation. Had there been a passage concerning Limbo? No, there had not; and there had been no Dormant Souls, though perhaps he had touched on the Last Judgment. He wasn't sure. Hell? It didn't strike him as probable, and all the same he had the impression of having debated at length on Hell, and of having placed the reality of Hell at the pinnacle of his investigation. On arriving at his home's front door, he broke out in a cold sweat. Of what, really, had he demonstrated the existence? Because something surely had proved itself to be indisputably true, unassailable, and yet impossible to fix into an unforgettable formula. Only then did he note that he was gripping his front-door key in his fist, and with a gesture of tardy desperation hurled it out into the middle of the empty street.

FIVE

A man who had not killed
anyone was sentenced to death for murder; he was
said to have killed, for reasons of financial self-interest,
a business partner whose private conduct he intended neither to explain nor to comment upon. All
things considered, he could see it might easily have
been his fate—since the person in question had been
his partner—to receive a more opprobrious condemnation. The judges had even admitted evidence that
he, the condemned man, had been ignobly swindled.
In truth, even while having been certain of it, he
had never attempted to determine if he had been
swindled, or to what degree. He had mentally accepted the figure of two-thirds as a reasonable ap-
proximation. In actual fact, as he discovered at the
trial, the fraud had been far smaller. In this sense,
the trial had cheered him up; it had given him the
certainty of his friend's having been a cheat, but to
discover that he also had been timid and restrained
had been profoundly moving. The man attempted to
explain that he had been convinced of having been
swindled of two-thirds, and all the same had never
contemplated murder. How could he have killed for
so small a wrong? It was useless; he heard it pronounced that his personality was flawed, and that
he suffered from delusions of omnipotence. All the
same, he was not insane even though, more than an
inclination, he had a kind of love for insanity. He saw

that the observation was not ungrounded. From that moment on, he made no attempt to defend himself in any rational or properly argued way. For it to have been his lot—a man mild-mannered to the point of slothfulness—to end up in court, accused of homicide, struck him as so wondrous and improbable as to lead him to conclude that he had realized one of his life's great themes: the achievement of an objective insanity, not only his own, but a structural insanity, in which everything is firmly interconnected, perfectly deducible, perfectly concluded. Delusions of omnipotence? He was truly omnipotent. Since he, the innocent party, had been held to be guilty of homicide, he, and he alone, was the cornerstone of the whole demented structure. What a difficult role: he could not lie, since finally he had found his way into a world of true reality; nor could he simulate madness without endangering the entirety of the edifice of madness. Considerable cunning would have to be brought to bear, and he was quite well-stocked.

SIX

A man who knows Latin but no longer Greek paces back and forth in his home, and is waiting for a telephone call. In reality he does not know what phone call he is waiting for, nor if it will come. Supposing that it will not come, he has no idea what that will mean. Certainly he is waiting for phone calls from persons who have something to do, in intimate ways, with his life. He is afraid of some of these phone calls. He knows that he is easily cornered, and that for a little bit of silence he is willing to pay with his blood. For reasons he has never entirely deciphered, he has the sensation of being the object of intermittent assaults of hate and mistrust, which are feelings that give to those who feel them a considerable sense of potency, and which drive them toward the use of the telephone. He had received a phone call once from a friend to whom he had lent some money. The money, borrowed three years previously, had never been returned, but a profound hatred had arisen from it. His friend had even attempted to punch him. On another occasion he had tried in vain to halt the flow of a phone call sobbed out by an abandoned woman who had dialed a wrong number. With her, he had opened a telephonic correspondence which continued for a number of weeks, until at the other end of the line an unknown voice had responded, cantankerous and innocent. He had not had the courage to phone again. Now, he might be called by a woman whom he loves, but who lacks the courage to love him, unless with tormented interruptions. Or by a woman whom he loves, and who returns his love, but who is much too busy to be able to realize it. Or by a woman he does not love, who instead loves him, and who flatters him while never inciting unwanted and intolerable conflicts. In reality, he'd like to receive a different kind of phone call, unforeseeable, and destined to alter the image of a life he does not find to be interesting, but only irritating. He remembers the story of a friend of a friend who received a phone call from his father, six years dead: it was a rather curt phone call, his father having always had a foul disposition, and all in all brief and futile. Perhaps it had been a joke. The man who knows Latin would like not to be waiting for phone calls; phone calls come from the world; in conclusion, they are the only proof allowed him of the world's existence. But not of his own.

SEVEN

The gentleman dressed in a dark suit, and whose step is attentive and thoughtful, knows he is being followed. No one has told him so, and there is no proof of it, but all the same he knows, with total certainty, that someone is following him. He knows nothing about the pursuer but he knows the pursuit to have started some time ago, just as he knows there's a reason for it, even if only the pursuer is acquainted with it; and he knows the pursuit to be carried out with meticulous care and tenacity. Concerning this pursuit he could say little more: first of all, that he is followed less when he finds himself in the open, in crowds, than when at home. He doesn't mean that the hunt slackens, that the hunter is hampered by the crowd, but that the hunt undergoes a kind of diminution, almost as though a change took place in the space in which it operates. The gentleman also knows that the chase is very fast, and that since his gait is slow, he will inevitably be overtaken, and indeed, that he ought already to have been overtaken, and already there should have occurred what cannot help occurring when someone is overtaken; what that is he does not know. He does know, however, that the pursuer will never reach him, not even if he stops to sit on a bench, pretending to read the newspaper, in total surrender and unprotected expectation. The pursuer knows that on reaching him he would cease to be the pursuer, and the scheme of creation holds no possible place for him except as a pursuer. When the gentleman is at home, the clamor of the hunt, of the closing pursuit, the pounding of innumerable feet, deafens him; he cannot hear the sound of turning newspaper pages, he speaks out loud in order to be able to hear himself. In reality, in this rigorous and perhaps archaic division of roles, the person pursued, even while knowing himself to be unreachable, can never be free of the awareness of being a target. He knows that space deforms itself behind his back, so as to frustrate any hope of reaching him; but he also knows that time is not his ally. The only purpose of such deformations is to safeguard the function of the target. The target asks himself whether the pursuer is unhappy, since the horror of their mutual condition lies in an unperformable task. He wonders if there's a way suddenly to turn around, and to begin to pursue the pursuer.

EIGHT

The gentleman dressed in white grows suddenly aware of the absence. He has lived in this house for many years, but only now, as his sojourn most likely is drawing to its close, does he note that there is a zone of absence in a half-empty room. The half-empty room, all things considered, is just like all the others; and if it weren't for the absence no one would take any heed of it. The absence, of course, has nothing to do with its emptiness. A totally empty room can be devoid of absence; and one doesn't create a true and proper absence even by rapidly moving a piece of furniture. That won't create anything. So, this gentleman who is no longer young, who has lived in this house for many years, who has walked across that room innumerable times, has discovered now that there, in that corner, is not an emptiness, but an absence. He also knows he has often walked through it, and he knows himself to be involved with that absence, but he doesn't know how. He inspects the absence, and of course does not much understand it. All the same, something about his life in this house now seems to him to be less clear. It is well known that absences are reluctant to change address; and perhaps the need for the company of that absence had induced him year after year to prolong a stay in a house he does not love, among furnishings which are alien to him. Everything in this house is alien to him, except the absence. The

absence is so important that he could give up everything that makes his life tolerable—though in fact
it is not tolerable—simply so as not to be forced to
absent himself from the absence. He is tempted, of
course, to ask himself a wide variety of even con-
flicting questions about that absence. Human lips
are always ready to utter "What's this all about?"
But the man has not grown old in vain. He methodically erases his every desire to interrogate, to know,
to investigate. Light or shade makes no difference to
him, like love or abandonment. He knows that the
absence is indifferent to him, but he also knows this
indifference to be of such importance that without it
he would utterly despair. Only this surprises him: to
have discovered so late, at the end of the game, that
he had never been abandoned, as he had believed
himself to have been, but instead had always cohab-
ited with an indifference that he now regards as the
explanation of his survival.

NINE

The man attired in slightly old-fashioned but not inelegant clothes is walking the last few meters that divide him from his home. His return had been delayed by a disagreeable downpour, a slight earthquake, and rumors of an epidemic. On the road toward home he had lost his way a number of times, detouring around enormous ravines, collapsing buildings, piles of corpses fed to flames, machine-gun fire intent on preventing the sack of the temples of the faith, rich with incredible treasures. On thinking things over precisely, he now remembers his return toward home to have started, yes, at least a few days back, but as he widely skirts a bizarre exploding automobile, he sees that the paper which he grasps in his hands bears a dateline of several years ago, and a headline referring to a glorious war that he knows to have been long since concluded, even if he does not know who won it. And, though trying his best to be reasonable, he can find no explanations that might befit his feelings of calm, decorum, and satisfaction. There is no doubt that his home may have been damaged, at the least, or that the epidemics, the earthquakes, the enemy incursions may have dealt misfortune to the members of his family. Even, moreover, if some caprice of destiny should prove to have spared that zone of the city from the afflictions which have torn apart what once had been his homeland, time will not have passed in vain. Everyone, starting with himself, will have aged; perhaps some—but who?—will have died, uselessly beseeching his return, perhaps even suspecting for their own part that he may be dead or dying. A vague smile sheds a rapid grace upon a face more cunning than intelligent. His memories may be confused, but he is nonetheless certain of having done justice to a number of tasks with which he had been entrusted—humble tasks, since frequently they entrust him with simple and slightly degrading chores. He has delivered the bundles of papers, and there where he found some gaping hole instead of the house to which he had been directed, he had dropped down into the gulf the packages, the letters, the notes addressed to it. Where he had been instructed to await replies, he had waited a reasonable span of time and then moved on, upon beginning to suspect that remaining further might seem indiscreet. Only a few dozen meters divide him from his home, and by now it's night; the man foretastes the stories they'll be able to tell each other, and smiles.

TEN

The gentlemen who come to this station to await the train generally die while waiting. It is not a painful death; it is indeed quite calm, and, in its way, elegant. Some bring their families with them, especially their sons, who wear black knee socks and short pants: they're to learn how to die with dignity. Little by little as the gentlemen die, they are removed to a chapel adorned with the faces of many Saints, variously miraculous. Purely for the sake of courtesy, a railway functionary asks, hat in hand, if any of the distinguished Saints would like to resuscitate the corpse. He waits five seconds in silence, turns an interrogative gaze in the Saints' generic direction, bows, exits, and replaces his cap, because the station is incredibly windy. The wind descends from a crevice in the cliff, and no one knows from where it acquires that dry, foreign cold that makes the station, so they say, an extremely salubrious and restful place. It might be asserted that the gentlemen's deaths—and at times whole families die—confute this putative salubrity of the air. But in fact it's the general conviction that if they had not come up here, they would have died much earlier. Some would never have been born. In general, the wait for death is neither long nor unseemly; the company is numerous, people chat, there are games for both children and adults. The station master, a gentle and vigorous man, tousles the children's hair and nods salutations to his clientele. The trains that stop at this station are three: each comes from a different place and goes to another. Still, however, one has to consider that each of the lines is frequented by various classes of trains, some of which stop, or ought to stop, if the station master so orders. Others, the more important, never stop at all, and no prayer will avail. One sees the profiled faces, carved in wood, of people underway to a great distance. At times, a train that could stop slows down, and the engineer peers out from the window of the locomotive, scrutinizing the station master with interrogative apprehension; in turn, the station master directs a mute question to the public. The public make hand gestures, nearly as if to say, "Mercy, no!" or "Imagine that!" and look at the train as though it were transparent. The train accelerates, and once it has vanished from sight they come to carry away the gentlemen who have died, all dressed in black.

ELEVEN

A *gentleman dressed in* gray, and who when young had studied German—he still remembers a bit of it, and is proud of his ability to decipher the headlines of newspapers—is positioned beside a gray telephone. But, in reality, there is no kinship between them. Someone has told him to call a certain number, from which he will receive an important piece of news that quite directly concerns him. The voice that delivered this message was incontestably female, even if a little hoarse, and not unpleasant, though perhaps a touch embarrassed by a disagreeable assignment. Still, it's clear to him that the lady's words held no explicit allusion to a sad, dramatic and ominous, or even simply depressing piece of news. He is not even sure that the person in question was clearly apprised of the news; indeed, everything prompts him to conclude that the woman, whoever she may be, was entirely ignorant of the content of the message she announced. Moreover, if the woman or anyone close to her had been informed of the news, it would have made no sense then to direct him to another number. He has dialed the number, by now, four times, in two attempts separated by a quarter of an hour. No one answers. Now a second quarter of an hour has begun, and he wonders, without apprehension, what message has been directed to him. For quite some time he has received no other mail than advertising flyers from people selling automatic washing machines, or pamphlets aiming to give him explanations of the psychophysical benefits of faith in the true God. He is not hostile to the true God, but mistrusts Him. He is generally mistrustful of everything true, and has attempted to construct an image of himself of which it is hard to say whether it is true or false. He has no family, nor any friends of whom he'd deplore the loss. In reality, he thinks, while the quarter of an hour advances to a close, there is no such thing as a piece of news concerned with him, unless it's concerned with him alone, and no one else. If the news regards himself and another man, another woman, an animal, a thing, he will make it clear that there has been a mistake, and that what he has heard in fact is of no concern to him at all. On the other hand, it's entirely unlikely that another person, protected by a telephone or armed with one, will say anything so pertinent and uniquely focused. All the same, he is a man of discipline; he will obey that female voice and—uselessly, he presumes—he will turn the dial of the telephone which is dressed like him.

TWELVE

*A youthful-looking gentle-*man with the air of a person of median cultivation, a movie-goer with a love for film series, is waiting at the intersection of two lightly traveled streets for a woman he judges to be fascinating, gifted, and of delicate beauty. It's their first rendezvous, and he savors the dampness of the air—it's late afternoon— and takes pleasure in the observation of the rare passers-by, the ornament of his solitary thoughts. The youthful-looking gentleman has reached the appointment early: nothing would mortify him more than the thought of making that woman wait. His feelings toward this woman, whom until now he has never seen except in the company of people whose lives he does not share, are mixed, widely skirting desire while vividly inclusive of veneration, respect, the hope of doing some service she'll appreciate. It's quite some time since he has felt so rich and happy a mixture of feelings for a woman. He discovers that he's lightly proud of himself, and registers a shiver of vanity. In that moment, seeing himself caught up in feelings he had renounced, and for which he has no esteem, he realizes what he's doing. He has gone to a rendezvous. Nothing proves it, but this could be the first of a long series of rendezvous. As his forehead moistens with a light sweat of anguish and hope, he considers that at the crossing of those two streets a "story" might begin, an inexhaustible deposit of memories. Something tells him, brusquely: "This is the start of your marriage." He twitches at the sound of a woman's rapid footstep. "It starts now?" Few minutes remain before something in the heavens, in the skies of the fixed stars, in the balance sheets of the angels, in the *Volumus* of the gods, in the mathematics of genetics will begin to hum. She will rest her hand on his arm, and a road that will have no end will begin. An empty house awaits them, an obvious happiness, a slow decline, the growth of children, at first lazy, then precipitous. His face now grows cunning, its expression mean; he has remembered that he is a coward. He desires both salvation and perdition, and does not know which is which. He is a sleepy incendiary. The afternoon has turned into evening, the fascinating woman has not come. Beneath his voice he insults her; and when a timid girl asks him for directions, he pretends to hold her for a prostitute who has mistaken him for a client.

THIRTEEN

That gentleman *who is* crossing Independence Square and who holds in his hands the head they have just cut off is a Martyr of the Faith. His manner of dress is subdued, he wears no jacket, and his shirt is filthy with blood. That head he holds between his hands embarrasses him; he would never have thought it could be so heavy and cumbersome. If one were able—and many make the attempt—to espy the expression on the face of that severed head, one would see it to show the signs of a true perplexity. The gentleman, who seems to be making his way toward the stop for bus number 36/B, is in fact extremely confused, not so much from the trauma of decapitation as because it does not seem to him that he deserves the title of Martyr of the Faith.

The prevailing religion at the time of his childhood, and in which he had been raised, had believed in a God, in other specialized minor gods, and in various invisible beings, good and bad. There had been sins: no killing, do not give offense to cats, defraud no orphans, do not stick stamps on upside down, do not dangle your right hand, no cannibalism. It was an old religion which had known better days, but which with time had grown tolerant. Everything was forgivable. The Martyr had grown up in that religion distractedly, thinking about something else, and when the Others had emerged from the burrows, the discomfort he felt had been limited. But the Others found it fundamental to affirm that God was yellow, that the minor gods were hermaphroditic, that the Creatures were invisible only to the evil, to those predestined to condemnation. And their sins were, well, extravagant: do not rub the backs of dogs; coin no false money; do not lie except about sex, about which lying was compulsory. Had he perhaps said something concerning sex? No, not at all. Had he rubbed the back of a dog? In that moment, precisely as he reached the bus stop, the gentleman understood that he knew himself to be a Martyr of the Faith, but could not be certain as to which faith. Even the adherents of the old faith, since having been forced into the burrows, had in fact grown worse in character. For an instant he remained in doubt, but then he understood that his uncertainty embodied his prestige, his tepidity his strength: he stood at the start of a new career, when, just as he was stepping up onto the bus, his severed head slipped from his hands.

FOURTEEN

*T*he gentleman wearing an overcoat with a fur collar, and carefully shaven, left home at exactly twelve minutes to nine, since at half past nine he had a rendezvous with the woman he had decided to ask to be his wife. A man left slightly behind by the times, chaste, sober, taciturn, not uncultured, but of a culture deliberately not up to date, the gentleman wearing an overcoat had decided to walk the route that led to the place of the rendezvous, and to use the time for reflection, since he felt deeply that his life, no matter how the woman replied, was at the brink of a dramatic change. By nature apprehensive, he thought a dilatory reply to be probable, and would have found some gratification in a "no" pronounced with courtesy; he did not dare envision an immediate "yes." He had calculated a stroll of forty minutes, inclusive of the purchase of the daily paper, which, with its day-by-day reports of ferocities, was an object he considered tranquilizing: it persuaded him of his insignificance. Since there were three possible replies, he had decided to dedicate thirty minutes overall to the "no" and the "dilation," eight to the "yes," and two to the newspaper.

At the eighth minute of his walk, as he attempted to convince himself that a "no" would not preclude a useful and honest life, he heard the first, violent explosion. For quite some time, in fact, the pros and cons of a civil war had been much discussed in his country, but the gentleman wearing an overcoat, absorbed in the question of his personal future, had paid no attention. Even now he did not understand. Two minutes later, on seeing the explosion of the Ministry of Education, he began to have suspicions; and the tanks finally convinced him. He had a few political opinions, but somewhat bloodless. In that moment, his thoughts turned with virile apprehension toward his possible spouse. Things precipitated rapidly: at seven minutes after nine, the Prime Minister was physically defenestrated, three minutes later the President was jammed head down into a smoke stack, and the King took seat in the palace of his ancestors. He was an old king, and in a hurry; firing squads began immediately. The gentleman wearing an overcoat was shot at nine twenty-eight against the wall of an imitation Gothic church. They shot him because in his hand he still carried the newspaper he had bought in the early morning, when the country was still a republic. He was not unhappy to die; but he was slightly piqued by those two minutes he might have dedicated to the "yes."

FIFTEEN

A gentleman of dignified disposition has been informed that another gentleman, whom he considers a friend, has been the object of disparaging observations on the part of a third gentleman, whom the first gentleman does not know, during a conversation which had taken place between this third gentleman and a fourth gentleman, who's a fairly intimate acquaintance of the first gentleman; in truth, the source of the information was a fifth gentleman, who referred to it entirely in passing while speaking with the fourth gentleman in the presence of the first. It is also to be noted that neither the fourth nor the fifth gentleman is aware of any bond of friendship between the first and the second gentleman; the fifth gentleman also has no knowledge as to whether the fourth is personally acquainted with the second, and all things considered, that circumstance is of no interest to him. He is interested in the rumor as such.

The first gentleman is disturbed. He is witness to a disorder among his fellow human beings, and it would suit his sense of his dignity to attempt to medicate it. He might speak with the second gentleman, his dear friend, and assure him of his affectionate esteem. But he is not certain that his friend is informed of the offense, and he also has no knowledge of the nature of the relationship that holds between the second and the third gentleman, who obviously are acquainted with one another. He might challenge the third gentleman and demand an unequivocal explanation of his behavior. But he understands how hard it always is to come by any unequivocal explanation. So he will pay a visit to the fourth gentleman and speak with him at length, in an indirect but persuasive way, concerning the second gentleman. And he will tend, with caution, to encourage the perception that the fifth gentleman is perfectly extraneous, and uninformed. At this point, however, he recalls that the fifth gentleman is the very source of the story that troubles him, and, moreover, that paying him a visit would be useless, since he does not appear to know the second gentleman, and has no interest in him; the only thing that interests him is the piece of gossip itself, which cannot be laid to rest without appealing to personal references, which the fifth gentleman could not grasp. The first gentleman is very uneasy. At that moment the doorbell rings: it's the second gentleman, who has come to tell him that the fourth gentleman has ridiculed the first gentleman, of whom he declares himself a friend, during a conversation with the third, who does not know the first. As he speaks, the second gentleman cannot hide an interior mirth, a subdued amusement. The first gentleman is horrified by what he sees: then he shakes the second gentleman's hand, and feels a profound, liberated consolation.

SIXTEEN

The gentleman dressed in a linen suit, with loafers and short socks, looks at the clock. It is two minutes to eight. He is at home, seated, slightly uneasy, on the edge of a stiff and demanding chair. He is alone. In two minutes—by now no more than ninety seconds—he will have to begin. He got up a little early in order to be truly ready. He washed carefully, attentively urinated, patiently evacuated, meticulously shaved. All of his underwear is new, never worn before, and this suit was tailored more than a year ago for this morning. For a whole year he has not dared. He has frequently gotten up very early—in general, moreover, he's an early riser—but at the moment when all preparations were completed and he took his place on the chair, his courage had always failed him. But now he is about to begin. Fifty seconds remain before eight o'clock. Properly speaking, there is absolutely nothing he must begin. From another point of view, he stands at the beginning of absolutely everything. In any case, there is nothing he must "do." He must simply go from eight o'clock to nine o'clock. Nothing more: traverse the space of an hour, a space he has traversed innumerable times, but now he must traverse it as pure and simple time, nothing else, absolutely. Eight o'clock has already passed, by a little more than a minute. He is calm, but feels a slight tremor gather within his body. At the seventh minute, his heart begins little by little to accelerate. At the tenth minute, his throat begins to close, while his heart pulses at the brink of panic. With the fifteenth minute, his whole body douses itself in sweat, almost instantaneously; three minutes later, the saliva in his mouth begins to dry; his lips grow white. At the twenty-first minute, his teeth begin to chatter, as though he were laughing; his eyes dilate, their lids cease to beat. He feels his sphincter open, and all his body hairs erect, immobile in a chill. Suddenly, his heart slows, his vision clouds. At the twenty-fifth minute, a furious tremor shakes him through and through for twenty seconds; when it stops, his diaphragm begins to move: his diaphragm now grips his heart. Tears flow, though he does not cry. A roar deafens his ears. The gentleman dressed in a linen suit would like to explain, but the twenty-eighth minute deals him a blow on the temple, and he falls from the chair; upon striking the floor, absolutely without a sound, he disintegrates.

SEVENTEEN

The gentleman wearing a raincoat, and who every morning takes the number 36 bus—an always overcrowded bus—on which he attentively studies, absent-mindedly, a German grammar book, has in the course of his life been in love three times.

The first time, by now several years ago, he happened to see on the sidewalk the loose page of a magazine dedicated to sexual games, of which he knew nothing; by chance that page, in itself, was in no way lascivious, but showed the naked and nonetheless decorous body of a woman who worked for that publication. The gentleman—who on that occasion too was wearing a raincoat, but surely a darker one—picked up that sheet of paper, and when he turned it over his eyes were met by an extremely shameless image. He examined it indifferently, and returned to his contemplation of the woman both naked and serene. He instantly fell in love with her, even though not unaware of how silly it was to fall in love with an entirely substanceless photograph. The woman's name was in the caption, but he never made an attempt to get in touch with her. Rather, for several weeks he had the problem of separating the two sides of the sheet of paper, of comprehending that the shameless photograph and the woman he loved were at odds with one another, and, indeed, that, making their appearance on the opposite sides of a single sheet of paper, they could have no relationship at all. He never fell out of love with that woman, the emblem of incorruptible chastity, but one year later he permitted himself to fall in love again, with a woman he had met but with whom he had never spoken. It wasn't timidity: he wanted no response from her. Compared to the photograph, she was unpredictable, inconstant, and noisy. It was quite exceptional. He loved her form: not her corporeality, but the fact that, behind her, she had no other photograph from which he had to distinguish her. It was a highly beautiful love, and it brought him back to the religion of his fathers. He also began to visit the cemetery with great bunches of flowers, and to laugh out loud in front of his parents' tomb. The third time was simpler; he saw a woman at a bus stop. This woman was not only alive, but was also capable of making her way onto a means of transportation. That was the point where everything began: the lowest and the necessary point. In the grips of a desperate happiness, he addressed her, declared his love and obtained an astonished but courteous refusal. He thanked her, and went away, his happiness intact. His life had been extremely rich: and that had been the time at which he had started his rides on the number 36 bus, and his study of that same old German grammar book which he holds at this moment in his hand.

EIGHTEEN

That gentleman who has purchased a used raincoat and a floppy hat, who smokes nervously and paces up and down in a squalid hotel room for which he was asked to pay in advance, decided, ten years ago, that once grown up he would be a killer. Now he is grown, and no new fact, no love, no healthful early-morning breakfasts, no church hymns have in any way altered his decision, which had been no childish whim, but a clear and judicious choice. Now, a killer needs very few things, but they are special things. He has to have a weapon that's both prestigious and elusive, plus a perfect aim, a client, and a person to kill. The client, in turn, has to have hatred and self-interest, and a large amount of money. The difficult thing is to assemble these conditions simultaneously. Since the gentleman's temperament oscillates between the fatalistic and the superstitious, he is convinced that a real killer cannot help but find himself in the situation demanded; but he thinks as well, it being a complex and highly improbable situation, that it can come about not because the killer is competent and the aim exact, or because there somewhere exists a great hate or a terrible interest, and money for the killing, but only if something in the skies, in the stars, perhaps God Himself, if He exists, intervenes to summon together those scattered events which are often so distant from one another as not to be able to coalesce.

He wants to be worthy of a choice to which he does not hesitate to attribute the character of a destiny. So, having chosen a suit of clothes that might be a tunic, he has decided to perfect his aim. He is a novice, but has the vocation of an ascetic. He has immediately noted an error which all aspiring killers commit; they practice with fake targets. Fake targets do not test the killer's asceticism. This principle, in itself incontestable, has led the killer to several conclusions: he has made it clear to himself that he must learn perfect aim in perfectly ascetic conditions. He must not hit; he must kill. Not animals, which desire to be killed. Human beings? But to kill a human being without being given money is fatuous exhibitionism. A single solution remains, truly ascetic. He must practice his aim on himself. He has set up his weapon in a corner of the room, and has tied a string to its trigger. The killer meditates. He will now take aim at himself. And then? If he misses, he will live, but will be disqualified as a killer. If he acquires his mark, someone will be killed: the killer. He hesitates at length. But we know that his professional conscience will finally prevail.

NINETEEN

The existence of the heavenly body which we speak of here is improbable, or at minimum hypothetical; all the same, it has been sighted and described by habitués and inhabitants of space—tenants of comets, fallen celestials, miniature occupants of asteroids, prospectors of cosmic dust—not only in entirely similar ways, but with words regarded, in their respective languages, as distinguished and obsolescent. The celestial body has the form of a vast city square, its sides of approximately equal length. The pavement shows a number of peculiarities. It is mainly naked earth, with no trace of life: all the same, it comes to be called "denuded," since mixed with that clay there appear to be fragments of buildings, of a "No Stopping" sign, and even a fluttering, restless, fretful scrap of newspaper with a thunderous headline in an unintelligible language. It was witnessed by the "double" of a binary smuggler. The smuggler is said to have traversed a part of the celestial square, thus making another discovery which might have proved fatal to him, were it not for his singular duplex nature. The pavement, even though apparently solid and continuous, at times in fact abates into a foil so thin as to part beneath the footstep of a ghost; and below it gapes a smooth, empty shaft that opens down into the void. In a corner of the square, one finds what some insist is the imprint of a water pipe, perhaps for a faucet.

Gaps in the edges of the square allow one to think that other streets ran or will run into it. A comb has been found, along with a fingernail file of exiguous proportions. A dispirited pharmacist has declared himself, under oath, to have glimpsed a number of shadows, and to have heard low voices. In space, at the coffee shops, in the high class brothels for celibate gentlemen, discussions are held as to whether the heavenly body has fled from an odious city, or is the center of a city which still remains unbuilt; the voices and shadows would already have arrived, being more fleet of foot, in advance of the inhabitants, whose constitution is in any case corporeal. In reality, attentively observed, the celestial square shows contradictory characteristics; while appearing to be ruled by a pained but obstinate expectation, an impertinent self-assurance, it emanates at the very same time an odor of desolation, which might derive from bitter but unforgettable memories, or from a hidden expectation of catastrophe, perhaps of dispersal into space through the smooth tunnels by way of which the void presses so far forward as to graze the square's very floor.

TWENTY

That woman, there, dressed with precision, with cautious imagination, trusting more the rhythm of her limbs than the embellished impurity of her garments, that woman who is crossing the street, her gaze intent on the number of a bus she thinks she has to take, even though she is not sure, since many purposes await her, that woman is fairly young, even though I refuse to ask her any questions; and all the same, in the very act with which she crosses the street, aware of the ephemeral and neutral complicity of the traffic lights, captions explaining the course of her life attach themselves to her body. Perhaps you would not call her a beautiful woman, since you are ephemeral and sensual—odious traffic lights!—but you cannot avoid admiring the heavy and also guarded way in which she settles her body onto the street.

This woman has loved four men, and now administers a solitary but not unpopulated life. Three hundred yards remain before reaching the bus stop. With the first of her loves she had learned, still young, to fathom herself, through a dialog with a man of music. I hesitate to call him a musician. If perhaps a genius, he was surely vulgar, a sordid genius. Long discussions, constructed like great country houses, quieted the way she laughed, pacified her teeth. After that first of her habitants, she met a myopic and patient cybernetician; if the first had been a figure hastily sketched on the wall, years later to be rediscovered there, this one had been fatuous, vile, and eloquent. She tarried for love of eloquence. The cybernetician said to her "Wait for me," and crossed the street.

Two years later, on a day when the woman was intending to buy a zipper, she had an adventure: she does not know whether owing to love, distraction, haste, imperfect consultation of the dictionaries. A foreigner? She is not sure. She bore a son. There he is. Then she madly loved a tulip grower who played the lottery and believed that God has the hiccups. He regarded that son with suspicion, but no, not with hate.

Now that the woman is dead—she has already caught that bus, but that by now is of no importance—she walks among the dædals of the shadows and attempts to understand why her son, who survived her, in pain and alone, on the earth's strange curvature, was born from her adventure with a man whose name she does not remember. This is why he has that strange, tormented, interrogating face, the prominent chin, and a suspicion of laughter far back behind his eyes.

TWENTY-ONE

At *every awakening, every*
morning—a reluctant awakening, which might also
be described as lazy—this gentleman begins the
day with a rapid inventory of the world. He realized
some time ago that he always awakens in a different
point of the cosmos, even if the earth, the capsule
in which he dwells, does not look extrinsically modi-
fied. As a child he was convinced that the movements
of the earth through space direct it from time to
time into the near vicinity or even through the interior of hell, whereas it is never permitted to pass
through paradise, since that experience would render all further continuance of the world impossible,
superfluous, and ridiculous. So paradise must avoid
the earth at all cost, so as not to wound creation's
plans, which are meticulous and incomprehensible.
Even now—as an adult man who drives and owns an
automobile—something of that childhood hypothesis has remained with him. By now he has cast it
in slightly more secular terms, and the question he
asks himself is more metaphoric and apparently
detached: he knows that while he sleeps the whole
world moves—as dreams demonstrate—and that
every morning the pieces of the world, no matter if
involved in a game or not, are arrayed differently on
the board. He claims no right to know what this shift
may mean, but he knows that at times he can feel the
presence of abysses, the temptations of sheer cliffs,

or rare, long plains on which he'd like to roll—there are times when he comes to see himself as a spherical celestial body—on and on. There are moments, too, of confused impressions of grasses, and as well of the exciting but not infrequently unpleasant sensation of being illumined by several suns, suns not always reciprocally friendly. At other times, he clearly hears the sound of waves, sent by either storm or calm; and on occasion he is brutally reminded of his own position in the world: for example, when cruel and attentive jaws take him by the back of the neck, as must have happened countless times to doomed and exhausted forebears between the teeth of beasts whose faces they never saw. He learned some time ago that you never wake up in your own room: he has concluded in fact that there are no such things as rooms, that walls and sheets are illusions, a fakery; he knows that he is suspended in the void; that he, like every other person, is the center of the world, from which infinite infinities radiate. He knows he could not hold his own in the face of so much horror, and that the room, and even the abyss and hell, are inventions intended to defend him.

TWENTY-TWO

The slightly near-sighted
gentleman with a speech defect, and who smokes
a pipe, resides in the same building as a taciturn,
reserved, thin, and fundamentally young woman.
Both the gentleman and the woman live in decorous solitude, even if the home of the woman is
burdened by too much order, and that of the man
by too little. They encounter each other practically
every day, a rapid and casual encounter, with a faint
smile, a half-uttered greeting. Each has considered
the fact of the other in a number of ways. Free of
daydreams, without love, and all the same at length.
Each is lightly, but not unpleasantly disturbed by the
presence of the other. Neither has ever thought that
so occasional an acquaintanceship might give rise to
a more specific, more amicable dialogue. They in fact
have no desire to know one another, or to talk with
one another. Nonetheless, the absolutely minimal
problem that each of them presents to the other
does not cease to disturb, ignorably but constantly,
their lives. Each, moreover, has attempted to fathom
what has happened, how that off-hand acquaintanceship began, and what might be the meaning of that
annoyance, that torment which each of them repre-
sents, and both know themselves to represent, in the
life of the other. Each knows, in fact, that the other
feels somehow touched, somehow grazed, and considers this feeling a bizarre enigma.

The woman has concluded that the slightly near-sighted gentleman has some of the qualities of hallucinations. Thinking carefully, in silence, she has been able to recognize in that face, that gait, the movements of those hands, even in a certain jacket, traces of persons who have now been dead for years, irretrievable and dear. She has said to herself, partly laughing, partly in tears, that this man is a meeting place of uncles, parents, even childhood friends, and a man she had much admired and lost. The slightly near-sighted gentleman has attempted to change his schedules, routes, and habits in order no longer to cross the path of the taciturn woman, yet all for the purpose of assessing the nature of her presence. He suffered intensely, and senselessly. But he thinks himself to have understood that he is tied to that woman by a minimal but not severable bond, by something that links the most secret and unknown places of their lives. That tie is not love, but something that lies between shame and predilection. Both of them know it, but are not permitted to know it; each of their chance encounters is a harmless theft, but requires forgiveness.

TWENTY-THREE

*H*e *wakes up well before* dawn, shaken by the certainty of having committed a crime. His nights have been restless for quite some time, his sleep interrupted by frequent awakenings. In the morning his sheets are often twisted, scattered, as though he had fought for many hours against the coils of a serpent. The thought grows clear that during those nights he had been preparing a crime, a cruel and impious undertaking that now, this night, he has put into action. It is not seldom that his dreams disturb him for many hours after the night is over. He thinks that he has dreamed a crime, that the horror of what he has done has awakened him, that his memory of exactly what it was has been lost in the uneasy cemetery of unconsciousness. But he has not forgotten the sense of anguish, of alarm, and as well of potency that surely enlivened his purposes in a dream he imagines as long, intricate, labyrinthine, conclusive. Perhaps, he thinks, that dream will mark the end of his nightmares, and he will be able to rest in peace. Perhaps, in that dream, he played the part of the hired assassin who acts on the orders of a mysterious power. Nebuchadnezzar by now lives only in dreams, but continues, among the shadows, to commission atrocious crimes. He has killed, and now is safe. The King will give him no further such orders; the people of the sleepers is a horde of available assassins.

He is restless, gets up, wants to walk around the house, waiting for his body to quiet; he sees that he is trembling. He halts, horrified. A bloodstain oozes out from beneath a half-closed door. Is he dreaming? Has he left one dream and entered another? Or has a crime been truly committed in that house? Can blood from a murder in a dream flow even so far as to reach that patch of floor? He eases back the door. In the dark, he has the impression of glimpsing a body stretched out on the floor, in the middle of the room. He dare not turn on the lights. He looks at the pool of blood, which has spread still further. He retreats, takes shelter in his bedroom, trembling. What beats against the window panes? The wind, a night-time bird, the limb of a tree, a hand? Suddenly he remembers his dream. A great bird with a woman's face traverses a night sky and moves in his direction, noiselessly, extremely slowly. The face he sees is attentive and patient. But a broad wound drips blood along one cheek. That face has been in combat, and will fight no more. He now understands his restless nights, and the utter distress of that dream. He abruptly turns on the lights, and the spot of blood is gone; he throws open the door, nothing is there, no corpse, a half-closed window.

TWENTY-FOUR

T*he gentleman with the*
coal black and attentively scissored moustache is,
at four o'clock in the afternoon, in pajamas. From
time to time he lies down on his bed, from time to
time he drags himself about the house, and finally
he stretches out in a resigned and comfortable easy
chair. He turns the pages of a book, and doesn't take
a look at its title until after having skimmed a page.
It's never a book worth reading. Properly speaking,
he is not ill, he has no fever; but he has decided he
has the right to behave as though he were ill. He
is a graceful soul, but today has capitulated to a
solitary clumsiness. He is an easy talker, but today
is taciturn. Whoever phones him remains thrown
off by his voice, which evinces glassy highs, lightly
hysterical. The gentleman wearing pajamas might be
under the influence of a nasty bout of drunkenness;
but, in fact, last night, he drank moderately. All the
same, his intelligence, never exceptional, has lost its
edge; nothing interests him, and he has the impression of being in the house of a stranger. Perhaps it's
the weather's fault, which for several days now has
been oppressive, wet, without light. Or perhaps his
body, no longer young, is preparing for some sickness; or a sickness, having started already months
ago, has only now reached his body's surface. He
asks himself these questions indifferently. He is not
a superior human being; but today he finds it impos-

sible to look with exact attention even at his own possible illness. He peruses the corners of a table with toilsome interest, and finds himself thinking that in a wise society tables would have no corners—or should one say edges? No, it's wardrobes that have edges. In any case, there should likewise be no edges. Books should be spherical: balls with writing inside them. He giggles, and then feels a bland shame. He thinks he's being silly, and would like to feel piqued with himself; but even this is too much for him. He accosts himself severely, and asks himself why he doesn't attempt to live the role of a "positive hero." It's probably his father's fault; he has been told that his father drank. Fathers who drink have sickly sons. He thinks back to his father, indifferently ponders two or three moments, retrieved by chance, from his childhood. He is sleepy, but not, he knows, with the call of nighttime sleep, the sleep of dreams, and wheeling visions and repose. But, as well, it's not the sleep of death. He feels himself too silly for that; he's not up to so much. "The silly also die," he tells himself, as though to offer himself some comfort. He shakes his head, as if remarking, "The things people say."

TWENTY-FIVE

The gentleman dressed in a slightly rumpled blue suit, and who at this moment is crossing the badly lit street, his footstep slightly tottering, is in fact completely drunk, and his goal is simply to get back home. It is not remarkable for him to be drunk, though in general he decorously holds his wine; the remarkable thing is the type of drunkenness from which he suffers. In general, he turns argumentative, obstinate, captious, and easily takes offense; he insults unassuming women, and turns his eyes toward municipal policemen with a certain timid arrogance. He makes nasty remarks about horses, and insinuations concerning dogs. In general these are moments in which he is convinced of living in a sordid society that deserves to be loathed and ridiculed. Tonight, thanks to that body of occult laws which not infrequently guide a series of debaucheries, he has come to regard himself as a part of that world which deserves contempt. He is responsible, and Tibet, original sin, and the class struggle all clash with one another in his chaotically brightened mind. Would he still have time for a new life? What example does he give his children, coming home drunk like this? And does his poor wife deserve so debased a husband? He likes "debased," and it strikes him as a good definition; it also fits a man on the verge of self-redemption. For example: he will walk in the night until boiling off the most repugnant part of his drunkenness; then he will go home to talk with his wife, whom he respects and holds dear; he is not one of those men who find their wives tiresome owing simply to seeing them every day. In that moment, the din of a passing tram that overtakes him from behind reminds him of something. But of what? He concentrates. My God! Hadn't he killed his wife precisely that afternoon, striking her across the skull with an iron pipe? The screams. The gentleman makes a gesture of horror, clasping his hands over his ears. He laughs. He's shrewd. He will not go home. Or turn himself in, or become a monk. The night air suddenly gusts against him. He remembers that he has no wife. So, what use are good resolutions for a man who has no wife? And how could one murder such a wife? Holding steady, insofar as he can, he attempts to fathom why he has no wife. Everybody has one. So what does that make of him, a dog? How did his wife conspire not to marry him? Or is it he who did not marry her? The day before the wedding, she ran away with an heretical priest. But isn't he that priest? That woman ran away with him? Or with another? Who ran away? "The bitch," he says, and searches in his pocket for his keys, his eyes wet with tears, as his face curls up in a grin of contempt.

TWENTY-SIX

Like all sick people, he of-
ten wakes up in the morning with a deep, unbounded
sense of health. He is unaware of how the world has
closed down around him, of the brevity of the paths
he travels even inside his own home. His ever more
minuscule life seems to him just the right size, a suit
that fits his limbs with elegance and propriety. Why
go out when the sky is low with clouds, and there is
no sign of the sun? Why move at all, when remaining
still is clearly so much more to the point and insight-
ful? He feels well, so why should he make movements,
or speak words, or think thoughts that might make
that admirable sense of equilibrium vacillate?

But other persons are in motion around him;
it's in them, he perceives, that the danger lies. He
would like to be alone, but he also knows that the
solitude that best protects him must be patiently created and held in place within a crowd: at least three
or four persons. His wife observes his face: "You're
really much better, you know," she comments. The
perfect equilibrium has been broken, miserably shattered. He looks in the mirror at that face, perused by
barely a glance from a wife who for years has lived
with him and that face, who has grown accustomed
to his existence, thus exercising a habit that he has
not managed to contract. He examines the face that's
better: thin, the unnaturally large eyes, the dry lips
no one would presume to kiss, consecrated to some-

thing else. He looks at the skin of his neck, that disheveled hair. He lies back down again, directing his thoughts to his body, that body which for one brief instant he had forgotten himself to wear. Perhaps he is better, he inwardly smiles. The problem of life, he preaches to himself, glaring at himself, like a drunken preacher, is "never to stop getting better, uninterruptedly, day after day, hour after hour." One starts getting better with the first scream after birth—the beginning of the convalescence! "Take good care of the baby." He too has had a son, but the boy has never said to him, "You're better." His gaze, of course, lacks subtlety, distracted as it is by rapid youthful passions. The sick man laughs. He's getting better day by day, that's clear to see. Still a bit more to go; ever less. One of these coming mornings—soon he'll be able to start to count—he'll wake up wholly free of symptoms; forever, finally.

TWENTY-SEVEN

A *man who owned a horse* of unaccustomed elegance, a fortified dwelling, three familiars and a vineyard, believed himself to have understood, from the attitude taken by the clouds around the evening sun, that he had to depart from Cornwall, where he had always lived, and travel to Rome, where, he supposed, he would have the opportunity to speak with the Emperor. He was neither superstitious, nor an adventurer, but those clouds had made him wonder. He spent no more than three days making preparations, wrote a nondescript letter to his sister, an even more nondescript letter to a woman whose hand he had thought, out of simple idleness, to request in marriage, made a sacrifice to the gods and departed, one cold, clear morning. He crossed the channel that separates Gaul from Cornwall and before too long found himself in a great wooded place, empty of roads; the sky was restless and frequently he sought repair, with his horse, in grottoes that bore no sign of human habitation. On the twelfth day, at a ford, he found a human skeleton, with an arrow between its ribs: when he touched it, it crumbled into dust, and the arrow rolled off among the stones with a metallic tinkle. After a month, he came to an impoverished village inhabited by peasants whose language he did not understand. He had the impression that they warned him. Three days later, he met a giant with a coarse face and three eyes. He was saved by his horse's lightning speed, and huddled for a week in a forest no giant would ever enter. During the second month he traversed a land of elegant little towns, crowded cities, noisy markets; he encountered men from his own country and learned that a secret sadness afflicted the region, corroded by a slow pestilence. He crossed the Alps. At Mutina he ate lasagne and drank foaming wine. In the middle of the third month he reached Rome. He found it wondrous, and did not know how greatly its luster had diminished in the last ten years. There was talk of plagues, of poisonings, of emperors who were either craven or ferocious, or both. Since he had come to Rome, he attempted to live there for at least a year: he taught Cornish, practiced swordsmanship, drew exotic designs for the use of the Imperial chiselers. In the arena, he killed a bull, and was noticed by a court official. One day he encountered the Emperor, who, mistaking him for someone else, looked at him with hatred. Three days later, the Emperor was stabbed to death and the man from Cornwall was acclaimed emperor. But he was not happy. He always wondered what those clouds had meant to say to him. Had he misunderstood? He was thoughtful and despondent. He grew serene the day the court official raised a sword against his throat.

TWENTY-EIGHT

*E*xcited *by a strange and* senseless design of the clouds at dawn, the Emperor arrived in Cornwall. But the voyage had been so strenuous, so tortuous and errant as to leave him with a very unclear memory of the place from which he had first set out. He had departed with three squires and a menial. The first squire had run off with a gypsy woman, after a desperate discussion with the Emperor during a night charged with strokes of lightning. The second squire had fallen in love with the plague, and would hear no reason to abandon a village devastated by advancing death. The third squire had enrolled into the troops of the following emperor, and had tried to assassinate him. The Emperor was forced to consider him condemned to death, and pretended to carry out the sentence by cutting his throat with his little finger; they both had laughed, and bade farewell to one another. The menial had remained with the Emperor. Both of them were silent, melancholy men, aware of pursuing a goal which was not so much improbable as irrelevant; they both had metaphysical notions which were highly imprecise, and whenever they came to a temple, a church, a sanctuary, they did not enter, since both of them were certain, for different reasons, that inside such places they could only encounter lies, equivocations, disinformation. Once they had arrived in Cornwall, the Emperor made no secret of his discomfort: he did not understand the language, he did not know what to do, his coins were examined with suspicious care by diffident villagers. He wanted to write to the Palace, but did not remember the address. An emperor is the only man who can, or must, be ignorant of his own address. The menial had no problems: remaining with the disoriented emperor was his only way of establishing orientation. As time passed, Cornwall opened to merchant traffic and the tourist trade. And a history professor from Samarkand, Ohio, recognized the emperor's profile: by now he passed his days at the pub, served by his taciturn drudge. News of the Emperor's presence in Cornwall spread rapidly, and even though no one knew what an emperor might be, nor with respect to what part of the world, the locals found it flattering. Beer was served to him for free. The village in which he resided put one of his coins in its coat of arms. The menial was given a generic noble title, and the Emperor, who speaks by now a little of the local language, is in a few days time to marry the beautiful daughter of a depressed warrior; he now has a watch and eats apple pie; they say that at the next elections he'll be a candidate for the liberals; and he will lose with honor.

TWENTY-NINE

But what are you doing here?" an astonished voice inquired of an elderly gentleman, dressed in a dark suit, and carrying an absurd umbrella. "Pardon?" said the elderly gentleman, with a foreign accent. "But are you dead?" "No, not at all," the elderly gentleman replied. "Are there dead people here?" "But how did you get in?" the first voice continued. More perplexed than irritated, it was the voice of a younger man by nature respectful of the elderly. "Please wait here for a moment," he added, and went off to talk with another young man intent on moving large skeins of a light, thread-like material. The elderly gentleman noticed that the two young men were dressed in the same pale blue uniform, slightly cheap, of messenger boys, he couldn't help saying to himself. The second guard approached the elderly gentleman, and was decidedly alarmed: "Now, you have to understand that this is something serious," he said, "nobody gets in here, alive." "Am I in hell?" the elderly gentleman asked, without sarcasm, but with much curiosity. "Oh no, oh no," said the good guard, "it's just that this is a secret place, you understand? Are you sleeping now?" "But of course," the elderly gentleman replied, "it's two o'clock in the morning," and consulted his watch. "And tomorrow I have to get up early." "So, he must have ended up in here by way of a dream," said the first guard to the second. "Shall we kill him?" "Are

you crazy?" the other snapped. "Kill the professor?"
"Well, you surely can't say that this isn't a fine mess.
By now he's seen everything. Shall we send him
back?" The professor perused them attentively, as
though he understood, and then again did not. "So,
you're Jewish?" the first guard said, with a cordial
air. The gentleman nodded yes. "What's needed here
is a good repression," the second muttered. "Just a
moment," replied the first, with a slightly Milanese
accent. He turned to the elderly gentleman, "Do you
know where you are?" The gentleman replied with
an ambiguous nod of the head. Then he added, "But
I ended up here by accident, through a dream." Another voice rang down from a railing: "I need those
incests!!!!!" "Holy ghosts," the second said, "the
incests!" and ran to his enormous skeins of thread.
"Have you understood?" the young man reverently
looked at the elderly gentleman. "You just go back
to sleep, but after this you're one of us." The gentleman showed the shadow of a smile. "You see, by day
you won't know anything, but at night, by now, you
know it all. So, we can't just let you go around like
that, wandering about by chance. You understand?"
And since that time, the professor, at night, takes on
minor roles in the dreams of the rich, partly playful,
partly threatening.

THIRTY

At ten-thirty in the morn-
ing, a heavyset man, bearded, and dressed in a
slightly rumpled suit, realized that he had the gift
of performing miracles. A very simple gesture was
all it took: rubbing his right thumb on the tips of
the index, middle and ring fingers of the same hand.
Naturally, it had happened by chance the first time,
and he had healed a despondent cat, instantaneously.
It was a question of miracles, not of "wish fulfill-
ments." When he made that gesture and asked for
money—he specified the sum, quite reasonable—
nothing happened. He had to be of benefit to someone else. He healed a child, quieted a horse, placated
the fury of a homicidal maniac, held in suspension
a wall that risked collapsing on grandparents and
infants. Disgusting: there was no other word for it.
He would never have believed that being a thauma-
turge could be—how to put it?—so *cheap*. There
was only one point in favor to the heavyset man, but
an important one: he was not a believer. He was not,
precisely speaking, an atheist, since he did not have
a philosophic soul; but religions—all of them—got
on his nerves. And why had this miracle thing happened precisely to him? Maybe we could call this fact
the proof of the existence of a supreme Power. But
what sort of power would it be? There were dozens
of gods, and demigods, demons, pixies, ghosts. He
wasn't interested in performing miracles. So, was it

all some kind of joke? An attempt to convert him? A way of "confounding" him? The heavyset man was irritated. On reaching the fortieth miracle, and the realization that news was beginning to get around, he decided to make a move. This was what led him to enter, with vivid reluctance, the church of a neighborhood in which he had never performed any miracles, and there to confront a priest. He made himself clear: he indicated not only that he was no believer, but as well that those miracles might come from a God entirely different from the one which that church worshipped. The priest showed no astonishment. "It's not the first such case," he said, "even though here we haven't had any examples. Are you married?" "No." "Why don't you become a priest?" "But I'm not a believer," he replied. "So, who's a believer by now? Look, you perform miracles: if you had a mathematical talent, I'd tell you to become an engineer." The heavyset man's penultimate miracle was to convert the priest and direct him to repentance. His last: his self-abolition, to allow the priest to convince himself that he had experienced the miracle of grace. This last of his miracles was much admired by the experts.

THIRTY-ONE

T*o be perfectly honest, this* man is doing nothing at all. He is loafing. He lies there on his bed, stretches, shifts position. He walks around the house. He makes himself a cup of coffee. No, he doesn't make himself a cup of coffee. No, he doesn't walk around the house. He thinks about the marvelous things he might do, and feels slightly ill at ease. It would nonetheless be exaggeration to call it remorse. It's simply that non-activity is a form of activity to which he is unaccustomed. If I were in the army—he thinks—and one of those soldiers who feels himself a man only when cannons roar, and there's a reasonable chance of death or mutilation, and, in any event, of being metamorphosed into a statue, I'd have to say that I'm behaving not only as though cannons were still, but nearly as if some universal peace had been declared, along with the destruction of all war statues. How would such a soldier feel? He'd feel entirely useless. But there's a fundamental difference: that soldier, in fact, most likely would be unhappy, and would end up picking a fight with a traffic cop who, thanks to his uniform, might be seen as an enemy. I—this man continues—am not unhappy. No, saying that I am happy would again be wrong; I am not that brazen. It's only that I find a certain cheer, let's say, in my chest of drawers. Now, my chest of drawers is a graceless and dilapidated object, and finding a certain cheer in it means that I treat it like a good dog that bites nobody and doesn't dirty the floor. I'm also fond of the little chandelier, despite its being a fake, and a little silly. I adore my slippers, which obey their fairly limited calling with inexpressible passion. Never were the feet of divas or saints held in such affectionate custody. Now, one can think nothing good about a person who confesses that he loves his houseshoes. He attempts, in fact, not to think. But to tell the truth, he cannot manage it. Properly speaking, one could not say that he thinks, but he has the impression that somewhere down inside him, some zone of himself which is generally deafened by other parts is thinking very rapidly, or formulating projects, or mulling things over—things.... Who knows what things they could be? Nothing serious. Or nothing true, let's say. But mulling them over with so much ability, speed, and cunning as to hold him apart from any possibility of guilt. For a few hours his only métier is to listen to the clock. But what clock? Ah, he really does not know. Not the watch he wears on his wrist, and which has always set the rhythm of his work. Perhaps somewhere a ticking sound is simulating thought, and measures out—for an instant it seems clear to him—hours which still do not exist, which have not yet begun.

THIRTY-TWO

That man is made of plaster.
He is of course a statue. He could even be made of
marble, but the City chose plaster, which costs less.
The man made of plaster takes no offense. Plaster
is not a many splendored thing, but has its dignity.
It gets dirty, which is a sign of toil and daily life,
and thus of a noble life. Being made of plaster, he
most likely has a family: a plaster wife in a park, a
couple of plaster boys in a private garden, or in the
entrance hall of an orphanage. It's common knowledge that marble statues do not have families. Marble
is beautiful, with fine highlights; clean, but frigid.
No marble gentleman has a marble wife, except in
those rare cases of having been forced, for dynastic
reasons, to accede to a marriage of state. The gentleman made of plaster is reasonably content with the
clothes in which they have dressed him: trousers a
wee bit tight, with a flapped pocket, one of the skirts
of his jacket with its corner raised, as though the
wind were blowing, a vest with all its buttons, of
which he is very proud, since a vest is a sign of a
well-conducted career. They have given him a book
to carry in the crook of his upper right arm. He has
no idea as to just what book it is, the title is toward
the street, to be read by the passers-by, though none
of them, in truth, ever do so, unless on occasion for
children intent on wasting time. He does not know
what theme that book discusses, nor if it's his, or if

they have only lent it to him. It annoys him not to be able to read its title; he has attempted to make it out on the creaseless lips of the children, but has never managed. He is also bothered, slightly bothered, by something else: he stands erect on a pedestal—he knows, indeed, that there are seated statues, but that does not disturb him—and something is written on that pedestal. It must be a name, and dates of birth and death. Being a statue, a monument, he takes no interest in dates. He is interested in the name, because it is the name of the person of whom he is the statue. He is content with being a statue, but why not tell him of whom? All in all, the important thing is to be a good statue, and to amuse himself with the pigeons that flutter up against him. What the statue does not know is that the gentleman of whom the gentleman made of plaster is the statue is furious. Him, in plaster! Him, a perch for pigeons! Him with that book beneath his arm! He, after all, wrote so many books, and so much thicker and more definitive! The gentleman is infuriated and, moreover, had always had a nasty character. Since his death, some twenty years ago, he has never taken a turn through that part of town. At most, when it rains in a stiff wind, he peeks around the corner of an alley, cursing the man made of plaster and hoping that he'll fall apart, that he'll crumble, and dissolve, him and his blots of pigeon shit. It's a shame no one has told him how happy that man made of plaster is to be his statue, and of how much pride that gives his wife, who is Clio, the Muse of History.

THIRTY-THREE

With time, he has turned into a passionate waiter. He loves to wait. Extreme in his own punctuality, he detests the punctuality of others, who with all their maniacal exactitude cut him off from the enormous pleasure of that empty space where nothing human happens, nothing foreseeable, nothing here-and-now: that space where everything has the heady, indefinite odor of the future. If the appointed meeting place is an intersection, he likes to construct a fable of possible misunderstandings: he moves along from one corner to the next; returns to where he started from; looks around himself; scrutinizes; crosses the street. Waiting becomes adventurous, restless, infantile. There was a time when a ten-minute lateness would send him into a silent rage, as though he had been affronted. Now he'd like latenesses of fifteen minutes, twenty. But the lateness must be real. So, arriving early is pointless. Sometimes the wait is stationary. He finds some object on which to sit, and he sits there, and dangles a leg, slowly. He looks at the toe of his shoe, which is something he could not do at any other moment of the day. As the wait grows longer, he shifts position, crossing his other leg, and studies his knee. Then he removes his hat and attentively examines its lining. Syllable by syllable, he distinctly pronounces the name and address of the hat maker. He replaces his hat on his head, then chats a bit with himself, as though between strangers who had only just met: he talks about the weather, fashions, even politics, but cautiously, since you never know where people stand. He loves to propose appointments in sheltered spaces, porticos for example, that allow him to walk about at length, savoring all delays with the slowly expansive pleasure of a master of a household awaiting guests, in the middle of a garden. During his waits, he in fact becomes the proprietor of the corner, of the street, of the designated meeting place. He takes up his position there like a host, and lateness is the natural gift that a generous proprietor concedes to travelers who come from far away, whereas he is—always—at home. If the weather is blustering up into clouds and wind, he suggests appointments in the neighborhood of churches. If rain indeed should fall, he likes enormously to repair to a church, almost always dark and half empty, and there to practice the secret piety of waiting. He counts the candles, nods a salute to Saint Anthony, with the orphan in his cassock, and gazes fixedly toward the altar, his body relaxed, without impatience, with a secret hope, projecting that allusion to waiting which is his masterwork.

THIRTY-FOUR

He is truly a man of habit.
He always wears, and has always worn, exactly the
clothes in which you see him now: a gray suit. He
has three identical suits, which he wears by turns. He
has three pairs of dark gloves, three hats. He wakes
up every morning at six fifty-five, gets up at seven.
The exactitude of his reawakening is overseen by
three synchronized alarm clocks, set to Greenwich
Mean Time. Another three clocks are in the constant
care of a single watchmaker, who is well aware of the
gravity of his task. At eight he is ready to leave the
house. He lives at the distance of a thirty-minute
walk from his place of work: he has renounced the
use of public transportation, of which the schedules
are inexact and unforeseeable. At five forty-five he
is once again at home. He rests for thirty minutes.
He reads neither books nor newspapers, which he
sees as charged with inexactitudes. He eats soberly.
He does not drink. He walks for an hour, inside his
house, or around his house, according to the weather.
He detests the weather, and considers it a sign of the
fundamental inexactitude of the universe. He repu-
diates wind and rain. At ten thirty he goes to bed. At
that point a savage struggle unleashes itself within
this still, calm man. He in fact detests all dreams.
Sometimes he dreams of dying, of being killed, and
finds it reassuring, since he supposes this to be a way
in which the "I" of the dreams is punished and de-

stroyed. He trains at forgetting his dreams, and persuades himself that they do not exist. Yet, the very fact that they do not exist while nonetheless possessing form, profoundly disturbs him. Non-being too is capable of being disorderly.

The course of his daily activities has become what he calls a "spiritual exercise." It consists of confining the world to the pursuit of the straitest of paths, on which ever less can happen. This "exercise," however, conceals a more subtle design, more obstinate and cunning. He wants to make his home and daily rounds a unique place, central to the order of the world. He wants the fall of his footsteps to be the world's exact pendulum. He is convinced that the world is incapable of resisting his exactitude. He has therefore come to cultivate an even more daring plan. One day he will perform an inexact gesture, incompatible with the world; and the world, he knows, will be torn apart, and will scatter like an old newspaper on a windy afternoon. Purified of dreams, the Void will be governed from the throne of God by the first-class clerk dressed in gray.

THIRTY-FIVE

That man is on his way to a woman with whom he does not think himself to be in love, while nonetheless fearing that he is in love with her. He is a cautious man, and therefore keeps careful watch on his feelings. He examines them one by one. None of them indicates enamorment, but continued examination, continued interrogation, imbues each with a coloring of guilt, which is not dissimilar to the blush of being in love.

That woman will open her door to him: she does not love him, and looks as well with great mistrust at every possibility of loving him. So, by way and even in spite of not loving him, she behaves like a woman who denies a love both to herself and to others. Both she and the man are subtle in the drawing of distinctions, and therefore are mistrustful of one another. All the same, they continue to seek each other out.

Their conversations are cultivated, and not untouched by a certain guarded passion. There can be no doubt that the subjects with which they concern themselves, and which here can be of no concern to us, fire them with authentic interest, abstract and mental. Both, in fact, are committed to their solid intellect: more robust in the woman, more volatile and capricious in the man. Both admit that the other is gifted with a rich and enjoyable communicativity; neither, perhaps, would know where to look for another, equally pertinent interlocutor. Their jealous custodianship of the severity of their feelings makes them tend toward intensely general discourse, acutely abstract, astringently ideal. They do not talk about people, they cite no living persons with whom they are both acquainted, they firmly avoid all reference to corporeal beings, as such.

They think it would be highly expedient to persist in these dead men's conversations, if it weren't for the problem of not being able to tell whether the dead know so much as no longer to have any need to converse, or whether being dead they are simply unable any longer to converse. When grazed by these sorts of thoughts, which they never communicate, they experience an ephemeral but not superficial anguish. They deeply love their conversations with one another. They love each other's voices, they love their argumentations, the doubts, the perplexities, the exceptions, the objections, the paradoxes, the syllogisms, the metaphors. With a bizarre, mental desperation, they think about a life that does not include the other's voice. And then, briefly, they fall into silence, since they direly mistrust, and will always mistrust, the vocality of the voice, that vain custodian of the purity of concepts.

THIRTY-SIX

The architect to whom the construction of the new church has been unanimously commissioned is not a believer. He is tolerant toward the ecclesiastic community, particularly the clergy; less so toward the faithful; in any case, he is not a persecutor. All the same, he is absolutely certain of the non-existence of God, and thus that the ceremonies performed by the priests are without objective meaning, and serve no other purpose than to distract both themselves and the faithful from awareness of the non-existence of God. The architect knows such words as "spirit," "soul," "sin," "redemption," "virtue" to be wholly without meaning, and all the same cannot deny his grasp of what they signify, at least to the slight degree that permits discussion with the new church's board of commissioners. He is a good architect, sober and inventive: he has constructed schools which are spoken of as "full of light," and "serene and welcoming" hospitals, a tactful home for the aged, functional railroad stations; the whole of a neighborhood complex which is the pride of the city that entrusted it to him. Now, for the first time, his task is the construction of a building he considers entirely useless, indeed mendacious to the very degree it is successful. The architect has a code of professional ethics. In and of itself, the construction of a church is nothing more than the construction of a building which is destined to particular uses, as specified by its commissioners. Now, these commissioners cultivate convictions that he considers not only senseless, but immoral; if they asked him to construct a gallows, would he accept without hesitation? But is a church a gallows? In a certain sense it is: it's a place designed as a station in a transit system toward the void. This is what the commissioners ask of him: that he adorn that place of transit. In doing so, he would be no different from the priests, who adorn that void and conceal it behind the veils of ceremonial fantasy. So, are they suggesting that he become a priest? He could be a priest of nothingness, an adorner who does not veil, does not conceal, does not elude. So, is that church a place of falsity, or a place of deception that nonetheless speaks the truth? Is there any other possible route for entering the void? "Adorn nothingness, construct nothingness, give us an eternal nothingness," he makes the priests say. He stretches out his hand and touches the unadorned grass of the empty terrain; and he thinks all at once of the altar, of the priests, of the grass, of nothingness.

THIRTY-SEVEN

The woman for whom he
was waiting has not come to the appointment. He
all the same—the man attired more youthfully than
suits him—does not feel offended. Indeed, it does
not bother him at all. If he were more observant, he
would have to admit to feeling a slight but indubi-
table pleasure. He can shape a number of hypotheses
on the reasons why the woman has not appeared at
their rendezvous. As he sounds out these reasons, he
does not desert their meeting's appointed place, but
only steps off slightly to one side of it, as though it
were a den in which some part of her, or the whole
of her, sat concealed. Perhaps she has forgotten.
Since he likes to think of himself as an insignificant
person, he is pleased with such an hypothesis, which
would mean that she too has identified him as exiguous, aleatory, and thus of such a kind that forgetting
him is the only way to remember him. She might
have reached her decision in a moment of caprice—
or perhaps of pique—since she is an impetuous
woman; and in that case she will have recognized his
function as a nuisance, as a minuscule bother, surely
no longing of the heart, but something no longer
removable from her life, or at least from a few of the
days of it. She may have mistaken the hour of the
appointment, and in that moment he realizes that
he is not clear, he himself, as to what that hour may
have been. But this realization does not disturb him:

he finds it natural for the hour to be imprecise, since he sees himself as having a perpetual appointment with the woman who has not arrived. Or has there perhaps been an error of place? He smiles. Might that not mean that she has taken repair, gone into hiding in some secret place, and that her absence is therefore fear, flight, or even game, a summons? Or that the appointment was everywhere, so that neither one, in reality, could fail the other, for either the place or the time? So he might conclude that in fact the appointment has been not only respected, but obeyed with absolute precision, indeed has been interpreted, understood, consummated. His slight feeling of pleasure is beginning to transmute into an overture of joy. He decides, indeed, that the appointment has been so thoroughly experienced that now he has nothing higher or more total to give of himself. Brusquely, he turns his back on the meeting place and tenderly whispers "Adieu" to the woman he is preparing to meet.

THIRTY-EIGHT

There is no doubt about his
being pensive, which is not an exceptional condition,
since he is a man who likes to think methodically,
lucidly, neatly distinguishing concepts which he han-
dles with professional expertise. In a certain sense,
he is pensive today about the fact of being pensive,
since his pensiveness has touched a theme which,
all in all, does not seem to him to be amenable, or
more exactly, which seems to him to be vitiated by
a fundamental reluctance to finding its formulation
in clear and distinct ideas; and this transmits to him
a vague malaise, which it is better however to lower
to the power of "discomfort." The theme is love. He
feels a lively, inconfutable interest in a young woman, who, according to a number of expert opinions,
shows manifest signs of being in love. Now, he is
entirely certain that his lively, inconfutable interest
is to be classed as a variant of friendship, of sup-
portiveness, of affective correspondence—a term he
finds quite satisfying—but as altogether extraneous
to love. All the same, he has the impression that this
young woman, in whom he does not deny a certain
prestige, both physical and mental, tends to propose
an inadequate interpretation of their relationship:
an interpretation which is not clear, not befitting, not
distinctly reasoned. This circumstance is a source of
embarrassment for him, since there is no doubt that
he regards the young woman's presence in his life

with undissimulated favor. On the other hand, for the respect he owes his own mental acuity, he cannot permit the young woman, who perhaps is somewhat precipitate, to believe herself to stand at least on the verge of a relationship; and he equally cannot permit that unclear thoughts be attributed to himself, such as not, for example, to institute a clear lexical barrier between "violent affection" and "love." He is absolutely conscious that within himself there is no love, no disposition to an intimate relationship, and that in no conceivable future is any such thing hypothesizable. He finds his position to be clear, honest, and explicit. He does not understand why the young woman finds it hard to understand such lucid propositions, and remains perplexed by his proposal of a non-relational relationship, not-loving but affectionate, warm but detached: a relationship, it seems to him, which at one and the very same time would embrace both clarity and utility. Moreover, he does not deny that the young woman's having fallen in love greatly flatters him; and that her disenamorment, should it occur, would strike him as an indication of inconstancy. And he would find it hard to be the friend of an inconstant and unclear creature. This is the point at which he grows pensive. He has the impression of having fallen into a trap of "unclarity," and he experiences a light attack of anxiety which will not come to an end until he has entirely, irreparably exited from it.

THIRTY-NINE

A shadow runs quickly among the fences, the trenches, the nighttime silhouettes of artillery; the courier is in a hurry, is guided by a happy fury, an unrelenting impatience. He holds a dispatch bag in his hand and must consign it to the officer in command of that section of the front, a place of many deaths, of many thunderous noises and laments and imprecations. The courier passes nimbly through the great tunnels of the long war. And now he has reached the commanding officer: a taciturn man, attentive to the nighttime noises, to the distant explosions, to the rapid, unlocatable bursts of gunfire. The courier salutes; the commander—a man no longer young, his face creased—unlatches the dispatch bag, opens it, reads. His eyes read again, attentively. "What does that mean?" he strangely asks the courier, since the message is not coded, and the words in which it's written are clear and common. "The war is over, sir," the courier confirms. "It finished three minutes ago." The commander lifts his face. And with infinite astonishment, the courier sees on that face something incomprehensible: an onset of horror, of dismay, of fury. The commander trembles, trembles with ire, with rancor, with desperation. "Get away from here, you carrion," he orders the courier: the courier does not understand, and the commander stands up and strikes him in the face with his hand. "If you don't get out of here, I'll kill you." The courier flees, his eyes charged with tears, of anguish, nearly as though the commander's dismay had been contagious. So, the commander thinks, the war is over. We now go back to natural causes of death. The lights will be turned back on. He hears voices from the enemy positions: some shout, others cry, others sing. Someone lights a lantern. The war is finished everywhere; there's no longer any trace of war; the meticulous, rusty arms are definitively useless. How many times has he taken aim to kill them, those men who are singing now? How many men has he killed and ordered killed, in the legitimacy of war? Because war legitimizes violent death. And now? The commander's face is streaked with tears. It is not true: it must immediately be made understood, once and for all, that the war cannot end. Slowly, with an effort, he lifts his rifle and takes aim at those men who sing, laugh, embrace each other, the pacified enemies. Without hesitation, he begins to fire.

FORTY

*B*etween the end of Sunday
and the early hours of Monday, he begins to arrange
the week, setting up a subtle, arduous calculus of
encounters. Generally, he dedicates Mondays, an ob-
tuse day that bears the unstable weight of a week, to
one of his five uncomplicated lady friends. He terms
"uncomplicated" the women friends who propose no
affective, sexual, or intellectual problems; women
he might decide, from one day to the next, never
to see again, with whom he had never experienced
an even innocuous weakness. He has five such uncomplicated women friends: two suffer from crises
of depression; one is nearly chronically anguished;
the fourth is absolutely stupid but ready to laugh at
his quips; the fifth is relatively well-balanced, but
too highly cultivated. The women who suffer bouts
of depression, when they are not depressed are, the
one, kind and delicate, sub-maternal; the second,
brusquely open and sincere, and slightly mannered.
The anguished woman when she is not anguished is
cautious, light, non-existent, subdued. Let's imagine
that he chooses the anguished woman and finds her
available. He cannot exclude the possibility of a late-
arriving crisis of anguish, and for the following day
will set up two appointments: with an outgoing and
generous friend, and with a placid and slightly banal
woman, utterly unacquainted with crises. He will
decide later. On Wednesday he would like to see a

woman he desires, but does not love, but he dare not speak with her before having set up Thursday with an extremely consoling woman who perhaps is in love with him, and to whom he will be able to entrust the inevitable trials of the preceding appointment, no matter what its outcome will have been. Fridays are masculine: he has three male friends, none of them authoritative, one a bit too intelligent for him, another prone to misfortune and therefore inclined to gratitude, the third boring, since he is in love, justly unrequited. On Saturday he will have to join some miscellaneous group, which in general accepts him while paying him no attention, but without ill-feeling. It's the anonymous day, and it's enough that he not be forced to dance. So, the groups he chooses are middle-aged. He seldom drinks too much; he enters no new friendships; he does not return home late. Sunday awaits him, the terrible Day of the Lord, if He were not dead; of the family; of sex. It's with a view directed to this hollow day that he has studied the course of the whole week: for the single, attentive purpose of postponing revelation and suicide, as he has patiently done since the day of his birth.

FORTY-ONE

The ghost is bored. It's hard, for a ghost, not to experience, for most of the time, a deep, slow sensation of boredom. He lives, of course, in a castle, which is in less than middling condition, and desolate. There are rats, owls, and bats. The castle is of only modest artistic value—a couple of balconies in flowery, fake gothic, an illegible fresco with one of the usual saints—and therefore attracts the interest of no one: neither ministries, nor scholars, nor tourists. Not even clandestine lovers: the path by which it's reached is lengthy, winding, and includes a decrepit bridge. It's entirely likely that the castle is fated to experience continuing decadence, and final collapse. It is also likely that the daily papers of this province where nothing ever happens every now and then run local-color pieces on the castle: the ghost has never seen them, and would like to know if they mention him, even if only as an object of superstition; he is not an ambitious ghost. A ghost can think things through, read, walk, and if sufficiently stupid or bored, make noises and shake drapes; this, of course, if there is someone to frighten. A ghost can leave the castle to which he has been assigned for a week at the end of the first century; for two at the end of the second, and so forth: a fairly bureaucratic affair. In theory, given the rapid displacements which are proper to ghosts, he might pay a visit to another ghost. But he does not know, and surely no one will tell him, where other ghosts reside. Moreover, twenty-eight years must still elapse before that first week-long leave, and it's really somewhat early for making plans. He knows that there are also ghosts in the city, but the thought of descending into such a place, after a century of solitude, fills him with horror. In theory, a ghost might come to visit him: but who might tell a prospective visitor, and by what means, that that castle is inhabited by an hospitable ghost? Hospitable? The ghost sincerely asks himself if in fact he is hospitable. Would he like to pass a couple of days, or a couple of hours, with another ghost? He wonders what they could possibly talk about. As formal as ghosts are known to be, most of their time would have to be spent on introductions. And once the introductions were over, the leave-taking ceremonies might well have to begin. But chances are that in that week he will not receive visits, nor attempt to make them. It will be simply a very nervous week, full of starts and stops and reputed knocks at the door, while waiting for the start of the second century.

FORTY-TWO

A man is attempting to
forget a woman; it is not an exceptional situation,
unless for the fact that he does not love that woman.
A woman is attempting to forget a man, a man she
likewise does not love. They have had no intimate
relationship, not even by mistake; they have made
no declarations, though perhaps they have shaped
hypotheses and imputed projects. The hypotheses
always took into account that the man and the
woman did not love each other, but all the same
were hypotheses that hinged on the woman and the
man. They have talked with one another about many
inconsequential things, and also about a few which
were important but extremely generic. No, perhaps
"abstract" is the word that's most exact. So, both of
them have involved themselves in an insubstantial
game of abstractions, devoid of emotion, but with an
intellectual potency that is intense. Are they attempting, then, to forget their abstractions? Each of them
knows otherwise. The torment lies in their having
discussed this game with one another, in conditions
of absolute non-love, and thus in having performed
a gesture in some way illicit, but in which by now
they are nonetheless caught up. They have admitted
to each other, laughing, that they feel themselves to
be chance accomplices in a crime which, basically,
was foreign to both of them: but, in fact, that foreign crime involved them enormously. Indeed, their

lives by now are molested by the transit of abstract figures, of elusive hypotheses which they can neither disperse nor compact: each has passed his or her own abstractions to the other. And out of a freakishness which is not rare, but rarely so minutiously elaborated, the abstractions have formed a system, have welded themselves into a fabric which now binds together this man and woman, even though they feel themselves, at every other level, entirely unattached to one another. But their very unattachedness is a part, indeed is one of the centers, or perhaps simply the center, of that machine of abstractions by which they both have been overwhelmed. They both—and they are not passionate people—have experienced the strange fate of being pushed toward a passionate experience that doesn't involve their bodies, or their use of words, or the future, or the past. Slowly, by mustering opposing abstractions, each erodes the other's image. But they're afraid of what may happen once that image is cancelled, once the figure of the other will have been totally expelled from each of their lives: they're afraid that web of abstract passion may remain, that freakishness of destiny which, having no face, is impossible to forget.

FORTY-THREE

The lily-animal, properly
speaking, is no animal at all; indeed, it is meek, and
even benevolent. The lily-animal does not run; indeed, to be exact, it can live out years in absolute and
minutious immobility. The lily-animal does not feed
on the flesh of living creatures, and all the same behaves as though having just finished its consumption;
it is said to have a kind of memory of tastes, which
also accommodates a trace of flesh of animal killed
and devoured: whereas, having no mouth or teeth,
in accordance with its benevolence, the lily-animal
would prove completely incapable of consuming
the flesh of creatures which have been killed. Yet,
notwithstanding these characteristics, the lily-animal
is known to students and is classified as ferocious,
fast, and carnivorous. The experts assure us there
is no other suitable way to describe it, even while
seeing that the lily-animal shows none of the typical behavior of ferocious, fast, carnivorous animals.
The truth is that it's common knowledge—whether
for scholars who examine the lily-animal in taciturn
slides, or from hearsay, and frightened, gluttonous
café chatter, no less than among the natives—that
the lily-animal must be killed; and that it must be
killed precisely in light of its being benevolent,
static, and continent. All of the qualities which in
theory might make it an innocuous, companionable
domestic animal endow it with a fearful potency,

fearful because insinuating, despite its being hard to say just how this animal insinuates. In short, it is ferocious not in spite but because of its benevolence; and those who nurture its benevolence will die of it. So, the paradoxical ferocity of the lily-animal is certain; and it follows that it must be killed. But killing it is difficult. It appears to have no heart to pierce, no head to sever, no blood to spill. Those who have tried to kill it with arrows, even with arrows made terrible with resinous fires—striking it is easy, since, as said before, it does not move—have skewered it but done it no harm. To approach its body and attack it with scissors—but what sort of body does it have?—is a great danger, since at close range the lily-animal can exercise its terrible benevolence. In short, there is no certain knowledge of any sure way to kill it. All the same, the indigenous population suggests the following: shoot off arrows while aiming in the opposite direction; or recruit a hundred youths who, one by one, remaining always motionless, smile at the lily-animal. Or finally—and this is the method most certified—one kills it in a dream, as follows: one takes the dream that holds the lily-animal, one rolls it up, and lastly tears it into pieces, without any gesture of ire. But it is very rare for the lily-animal to allow itself to be dreamed.

FORTY-FOUR

*This thoughtful and point-*lessly melancholy man has been living for many years, by now, in the basement, because the house that rose above it has been destroyed or is uninhabitable. When the religious wars broke out, he had hoped it was a question—he was a foreigner in that country and practiced another religion—of the customary depravities to which that region's inhabitants were inclined, all of them sanguineous of dying in some noisy and exhibitionistic way, and of killing others with particular cruelty. He bore no love for that country, where he lived as the secretary to the ambassador of another country, where wars of religion were not waged. His country fought atheistic wars, scientifically based. At the moment when the wars of religion had broken out, the secretary had been unable to return to his native land, where a ferocious scientific war was then underway: a war concerned, at least in origin, with hexagons and acids, but which bit by bit had then expanded to the inclusion of nearly all the disciplines, with the sole exclusion of ancient history. Now, the secretary, whom you see in sober dress, has been said, in generic terms, to practice another religion, but there is also the possibility that he practices none at all. What his country most respects is allegiance to ideals upon scientific bases; he himself, however, has no great love of science, and if he had to chose a field in which to specialize,

ancient history would be his choice. But since this is
the only non-controversial subject, choosing it would
have been regarded as suspect, and derided as cowardly. He would have been put to death. Fortuitously,
the outbreak of the religious war had allowed him to
give no response to requests for clarification that had
come from his homeland, but at the very same time
he had definitively exiled himself in the country of
religious wars. For years he had ventured no more
than a few dozen yards from his cellar; he was probably the only foreigner left in a country where massa-
cre was pandemic, and becoming pedantic; a country
that no longer had cities, but picturesque expanses
of ruins awaiting the death of the last combatant, so
as then to grow ivy-covered and be transported into
History. Though he had never admitted it in so many
words, he liked to live in that territory precisely for
its being the theater of a war that was alien to him.
So History was none of his doing, but was something perceived as a rumble to which he had grown
accustomed; as a lover of ancient history and dead
languages, he too looked forward to living—as had
always been his dream—in a country made only and
entirely of ruins among grasses that have no history.

FORTY-FIVE

Upon awakening, early in the morning, he must ask himself a question which he does not relish, and which all the same he cannot avoid: this in fact may be a day on which he will have to kill someone, or be killed, or kill himself. In truth, he has been waking up for years with this perplexity, but nothing has ever happened; he has not killed, he has not been killed, he has not killed himself. He might therefore conclude that his problem, as the saying goes, has been badly formulated, since its terms don't coincide with his day-to-day reality. But that's not so. His involvement with the problem of killing in fact is sufficient. Might one not, however, inquire about the point of view from which it is sufficient? He, too, has asked himself this question, and has found only one reply: that for reasons which he does not know he must be soiled with homicidal and suicidal violence; that he must be acquainted with destruction from close up, from very close up. Acquaintance does not necessarily demand that he strike down a human being, or see himself stricken down, or strike himself with his own hands: but he must be available, without repair, to all of these possibilities. Now, he lives in a solitary place, where, in effect, only suicide is possible. Which means that to kill someone he would have to travel to the city, at three days' distance: and meanwhile the order might change. But he is basically convinced that the order will not arrive, because what's of interest is not the effectuality, but the moral quality of destruction. For many years, he has seen his situation as particularly unfortunate, and he has lived in a condition of unnerving and depressing waiting. He has practiced the use of many kinds of arms, and cultivated the lack of pity. The lack of pity, all the same, has not involved the growth of any habit of hatred, and indeed has given birth to a kind of gentleness, a mild indifference that embraces all beings—homicides, victims, and suicides. So, he has shaped the suspicion of having been introduced into an operation which offers for inspection no more than its dark profile, and which evinces no trace of cruelty. Through living at the border of destructions, he had been placed, he suspects, on one of the edges of the world, and thus he is one of those rare individuals with the whole world behind them, expansive and unknowing, distant but eternal, like an infinite, motionless aura.

FORTY-SIX

The ghost peers out, dis-
tractedly, from the great, decrepit window of the
castle. It is night, and he contemplates the steep
slopes, the narrow valleys, dominated by his castle's
ruins. Through lengthy solitude, the ghost has grown
accustomed to himself, and makes no attempt to
abandon the ruins he inhabits, or to speak with other
ghosts. For a great deal of time, the misfortune of
encountering no others of his kind has distressed
him. He would have wanted to encounter a certain
ghost, someone he had known long before he became
a ghost—but by now the memory was confused. Had
there truly been such a time when he had not been
a ghost? Suddenly, in the depths of the valley, he
makes out something faint, and similar to himself,
advancing slowly, cautiously, perhaps thoughtfully.
And now a second pale light has appeared along a
steep pathway in the distance.

The ghost asks himself if, after centuries, two
ghosts might be coming to see him. He asks himself
why they might be coming to see him, by what stimu-
lus or from what counsel; finally, if they are coming
together or separately, and whether as each other's
friend or enemy. For the first time in many years, the
ghost knows anxiety and suffering. Who could want
so tenaciously to talk with him? And how, by way of
love or hate, had they found him there, closed up in
his castle? Finally, why have they come to seek him

out on one and the same night. Could one of them be
the Enemy Ghost, the other the Friend? And which
did he really want to see? Did he want to explain the
error that had generated the Enemy Ghost, or return
to the conversation, infinitely impossible to bring to
an end, with the Friend. Slowly, the two ghosts approach. But wasn't there as well, the waiting ghost
asks himself, a third, neither friend nor enemy, a
mediator, he can now no longer remember, but who
was that third, and as he died had he not perhaps
been torn between those two who now are ghosts, and
hadn't he too perhaps become a ghost, and is that
third none other than himself? So, could this night
see the reconstitution—if he hasn't misunderstood
what he is able to remember, if he hasn't been duped
by his hopes—of that threefold conversation which
wore them down to death? The ghost wonders if what
they told him in his infancy is true, that encounters
such as this one, for which he longs, gently consume
a ghost, and snuff him out.

FORTY-SEVEN

The dinosaurs were dying: the great reptiles were aware of it, and discussed, at an ever slower pace, the grand events of a history which had been great, glorious, never again to be equaled. The elders closed up into indolent conversation, or solitary meditation, conscious by now that no gesture they might make would any longer be meaningful, that no further greatness was reserved to them, that they could sin or not, nothing made any difference. One began the composition, in plain style, of a History of the Dinosaurs, written from the point of view of the dinosaurs of the final generation; but he came to see that his language, no matter how simple and unadorned, would all the same remain incomprehensible to whatever race might take their place in the governance of the world. The mothers and grandmothers wanted to hear no talk of the End of the dinosaurs; they took care of the last of the dinosaurs, played with them, taught them to pray in simple words for the dead who had gone before them, for obtaining the aid of the Celestials, and for living an innocent, industrious life. But the young bulls and the fathers tortured themselves with doubts: for what possible reason should the dinosaurs, the world's unchallenged masters, whose mass and placid violence gave them immunity from every other animal, be dying out? The Father Provincial, with creased skin and protuberant eyes, had laid the blame on moral lassitude, and alluded to celestial ire; the Free Thinker, smooth and agile, had spoken of a scant spirit of independence and improper diet; proposed remedies had included free love, the abolition of divorce, the introduction of the death penalty, the opening of the prisons: it was clear that no one understood anything, except that every New Year's Day saw on the face of the earth a smaller number of dinosaurs. They no longer raised discussions on borders, rights, duties, morals, nor on society. With resignation, with ire, with sadness, they spoke of the Celestials. They remembered that no one ever had managed to resolve the problem of the number of extant Celestials, nor even truly to speak with them. The best anyone had accomplished was via certain games with cards that a prophetess plied, still today, in the wetlands. The Celestials had abandoned them. Meanwhile, in the depths of the skies, the Celestials, unacquainted with sickness, were attempting to fathom the reason why they themselves were dying. According to the most widespread conviction, the blame lay with the dinosaurs, who had abandoned them, who performed no sacrifices, and had given up counting them.

FORTY-EIGHT

F*rom the moment at which*
he realized that it is impossible not to stand at the
center of the world, and that this holds equally for
him and for every human being, or animal, or even
stone, or alga, or bacterium, he had to accept that
there are only two solutions for a description of the
modes of behavior that this situation implies. If
the center of the world is active, the world itself,
endowed and enriched with infinite centers, will in
turn be infinitely active; alternatively, the center of
the world must be besieged by the world's totality,
or, more exactly, must constitute its target. At present he experiences the latter condition; he knows
himself to be psychologically spherical, and to
stand at the convergence of a vast number of radii,
which, strangely, concentrate themselves upon him,
or pierce him with their shafts of light. He senses,
in the empty hollows of space, the bending, without
the use of hands, of a bow of impossible stiffness,
and the shooting of an arrow that will reach him on
his sixtieth birthday. He attempts to shift position,
to fluctuate, but he knows that every movement of
his spherical body exposes him to the aim of other
constellations, of stars hidden by stars, of clouds
and animals. All the same, he is far less terrified
by any star or cloud than by always being in the
bead of nothingness and silence. He does not know
where nothingness may be, and suspects it is hidden

inside him. This would make him the target of an interior perforation, of a kind his sphere could not withstand, even though he does not know what this conclusion means; as far as silence is concerned, it results, as he thoroughly understands, from the suppression of all the voices which might speak to him in any definitive way, transpiercing him—and this is horrid—without the aid of any weapon. In every point where there is silence lies hidden a voice; and that voice thinks him, examines and scrutinizes him. If nothingness and silence ally with one another, if they exchange information with signs he cannot grasp, what will become of him? Oh, he does not fear the shaft sent flying by the centaur on the day of his birth, and which now reaches its mark. Him. He does not defend himself from the weary lance that crosses the world, directed by the will to wound him. But this disturbs him: his inability to distinguish between himself as pain, nullification and death, and himself as center of the world.

FORTY-NINE

A gentleman madly loved a young woman for three days, and his love was returned for an approximately corresponding period of time. He met her by chance on the fourth day, having ceased to love her two hours earlier. At first it was a vaguely awkward encounter; conversation, however, became more lively when the fact grew clear that the woman had likewise ceased to love the gentleman, exactly an hour and forty minutes before. This discovery—that their delirious love was in any case a thing of the past, and that presumably they would desist from reciprocal torture of one another with silly, painful, inevitable demands—at first imbued the man and the woman with a certain euphoria. And they felt they could see each other with the eyes of friends. Their euphoria, however, was short-lived. In fact, the woman remembered that twenty-minute difference. She had continued to love him for another twenty minutes, after the gentlemen—he had confessed it—had already ceased to love her. The woman found this circumstance a cause for bitterness, frustration, rancor. The gentleman attempted to make her see those twenty minutes as revealing her possession of an emotional constancy that endowed her with moral superiority. She rejoined that her constancy was beyond discussion, but that in this case someone had taken brutal advantage of it, and had covered her with outrage, cold and calculated.

Those twenty minutes during which, while loving, she had not been loved dug between them an abyss which nothing ever again would be able to bridge. She had loved a man who was frivolous and sensual, and in both this life and the next he would suffer the shame of it. He attempted to make the point that since they no longer loved each another, the problem might be seen as moot, and in any case was not of such a nature as to lead them to excessively bitter considerations. But he said it with a certain vivacity, which betrayed both fright and irritation. The woman replied that the end of their love was less to be seen as a comfort than as merely the indication that something loathsome had been fatuously consummated, and that she bore its scars. His laugh was brief, and not cordial. In that instant, a great hatred began between the two of them, a meticulous and overwhelming hatred; both of them in some way perceived that twenty minute difference to be truly something atrocious, and they felt that something had taken place which had made life impossible for at least one of the two of them. They began now to think of themselves as destined for a dramatic death, together, as they had fantasized, feverishly, when they had madly been in love.

FIFTY

He left the home of the woman he might have been able to love, and who might have loved him in return, with a sense of relief not free from bitterness. By now, it was clear that no love affair would ever arise between them, not even the poor and tepid bond of lust, since she was a chaste and robust woman; much less the languid tenderness of lovers slightly late in life, since that was not a thing that might for long hold interest for brains like theirs, in anxious pursuit of emotion. All things considered, he meditated, the impossibility of a love affair was a far better thing than the end of one. The impossible love affair, in effect, has something of the nature of fable, and transforms all the phantoms of hoping and waiting for love—hopes and expectations now totally disappointed—into a minor genre of literature, into something childish and, above all, non-existent. He, and perhaps she too, to a lesser degree, had conceived of a universe different from the one that was given, since, clearly enough, the universe in which they lived did not foresee their union: so, any thought to the contrary, given that it could not swell to heroic stature, revealed itself to be something futile, risible, even playful. One could also add that a love affair that doesn't begin will also never finish, even despite the clarity with which its missing birth holds a touch of the futile bitterness of a possible conclusion. But would he have wanted to live out a different story with that woman? The question, theologically, was an impossibility, and therefore demanded no reply, or only a reply of colossal proportions, on the order of saying: "I desire to live in a totally different universe, and I would find a sign of such a difference in the fact of being enabled to love a certain woman, and of being loved in return." So, the problem that kept apart their ephemeral bodies and feverish minds was not, despite appearances, a sentimental or moral one: it was a theological problem, or, to be more up to date, a cosmic problem. And from this point of view the problem annulled itself: indeed, in that other universe which God might have created, or in the parallel universe which might exist, perhaps that woman would never have existed: or, if she existed in a parallel universe of which she was a necessary condition, she might have been of such a nature that he would never have wanted her, and therefore would have had to spurn her, with recourse to subtle and perhaps insidious theological arguments.

FIFTY-ONE

The person who lives up there, on the fourth floor, does not exist. I do not mean to say that the apartment has remained unrented, or is uninhabited: I mean to say that the person who lives in it is non-existent. From a certain point of view, the situation is simple: a person who doesn't exist has no social problems, must endure no confrontation with the minute strain of stairwell conversations with neighboring apartment dwellers. If he greets no one, it is also true that he offends no one, and has no quarrels with anyone. For example, the apartment now inhabited by the person who does not exist was formerly occupied by a man of imprecise profession, but disagreeably renowned for his indiscriminate tendency to make himself a nuisance to every woman he approached for any reason. The embarrassing thing, however, lay precisely in his being in no way a reprobate whom a proper thrashing might easily have put in his place: he was simply a man who fell in love with unnatural frequency, whose intentions were always serious, and who wanted to set up a household, apparently with anyone, even with women who already had one, with aged mothers, with gray-haired grannies with loose tongues. In any case, the gentleman had been an embarrassment; so much so that one day he abandoned his apartment, and nothing more had ever been heard from him. Since it was only shortly afterwards that the non-existent person had taken his place, some wondered whether there might not be a relationship between the always enamored man and the non-existent person; some, indeed, even maintained that the non-existent person was none other than the always enamored man after death. But it was brought to their attention that an afterdeath person, or ghost, has nothing to do with a non-existent person. At first, of course, there was gossip, questions, curiosity. Later, the extreme discretion of the man who did not exist resulted in his going practically ignored. He made no marriage proposals, he displayed no unruly political ideals, he didn't litter the stairwell. In a certain sense, he was an ideal neighbor. And it was here, precisely, that uneasiness began: a vague misgiving that threatened the building's equanimity, the quiet of its tranquil, upright inhabitants. They all feel slightly guilty, since, unavoidably, they make noises, beat carpets, soil the stairs, chatter about irrelevant and perhaps indiscreet things when they meet one another. The impeccable conduct of the non-existent man is felt to contain a perpetual reprimand. "But who does he think he is, just because he isn't there," they murmur. It's clear: they have begun to envy, and soon will hate, the effortless, evasive perfection of nothingness.

FIFTY-TWO

The dragon, obviously, was slain by the knight. Only a knight can slay a dragon —not, for example, a career soldier, or a sports champion. There are knights who boast of the slaying of several dragons: they lie. It is not within the world's plan to allow a knight the slaying of more than one dragon. Even this is denied to many. Some, indeed, are struck down by a dragon, before the latter succumbs beneath the blows of another, predestined knight. The dragon lies mortally skewered, in a pool of blood but all the same bloodless, among snakes, frogs and snails; these animals do not denote the kinship of the dragon, but, quite the opposite, its total extraneity. In fact, the point which must not escape us is that the dragon is heterogeneous with respect to the place of its death, to the animals, to the sky, and above all with respect to the knight. Not much is known about dragons, but knights are generally ignorant even of that little which is known. Many believe that there are regions where dragons reside, distant and perhaps technically unreachable, and this seems likely. They depart from those regions; they always travel alone: no one has ever heard of a dragon couple, or family, or of two dragon friends. The dragon sets out toward the place where it will be slain. As far as is known, this is the only way of dying allowed to dragons. The dragon directs itself to the walls of the city, which in any case it never enters; it has no interest in city dwellers, but is searching for knights, since only from one of these will it receive its death. Sometimes a dragon goes off into a cave, makes it his refuge, piles up stones at its threshold. The dragon's mouth spews fire: which takes the place of its tongue. It is likely that the dragon has many things to say, but long solitude has made him unaccustomed to speech, and the intimate effort issues in tongues of fire. The striking thing, throughout the affair of the knight and the dragon, is the knight's absolute obtusity concerning the dragon. He does not cull its distances, its solitude, the enormity of its twisted mass; he doesn't decipher the signs of its fire. He is ignorant of the trials the dragon has chosen to face in order punctually to arrive at a terrible appointment. The knight does not know that he himself has arrived at an appointment. If, firmly seated on his handsome steed, he rested his spear against the ground, holding it gently, without ire or fear, the dragon, seeing his craving for death go disappointed, might perhaps open discussion.

FIFTY-THREE

This is not a properly hu-
man place, in the sense that its inhabitants are not
human beings, and that their notions concerning humans are vague, transmitted by ancient story-tellers,
or invented by merchants, geographers, falsifiers of
photographs. Many who possess a relatively higher
level of culture do not believe in the existence of human beings. They say it's a question of an old and
fairly silly superstition, and in truth the conviction
that human beings exist is mainly current among the
lower classes. Children, too, believe in the existence
of human beings, with the result of there having
arisen a dense body of fables which describe their
protagonists as men. The actions of the humans in
these fables are quaint and droll, but all the same in
their own way sinister; the humans weave unreasonable though rational plots. But the most singular
and vivacious industry to have been inspired by the
tradition of tales about human beings is the making of masks and puppets. Finely crafted objects are
produced and sold not only for the delight of the
children, but also as ornaments for the homes and
palaces, even of those who, having studied, do not
believe in the existence of men. These masks and
puppets cannot, of course, reproduce the features
of human beings, which no one has ever seen, and
which perhaps do not exist. Recourse must therefore
be taken to the various traditions, to old, absurd pic-

ture books, and finally to imagination. So the faces given to human beings always have holes through which to see, generally two, but randomly placed, one at the summit and one at the feet, or in the middle, which is to say in the midriff. Humans have an upper part which is circular or square in form, with at times another part attached to it, and members below for grasping and walking. From somewhere or other they emit sounds by way of which they communicate: and here the artists' imaginations take free rein. There are those who fashion trumpets that emerge in tufts from the humans' summits, or holes arranged as on flutes and ocarinas. For hearing, they have a kind of cartilaginous orifice, situated anywhere. Puppets that represent "sick" human beings are particularly popular, even though it is difficult to imagine diseases of the imaginary. Some are covered with boils, with sores, secreting vital fluids. They have cavities through which they cannot see; chipped flutes that emit no sounds; members that do not touch, that neither grasp nor ambulate. All the same, some suppose human beings to be immortal; they venerate those masks and puppets, and if they judge them imperfect or disrespectful, they reverently burn them.

FIFTY-FOUR

The ghost who wants to escape from solitude can do so only by generating another ghost from within himself. But even though it is known that such a thing is possible, there are no full accounts on this form of generation. The ghost not only desires to generate a ghost, but feels that he cannot avoid it—almost as though within his unreal body another unreal body has begun to grow. All the same, he does not know how he can help it to grow it, or how to make it issue from his body. He knows that giving birth to ghosts is a privilege few ghosts receive; and that the path to its attainment is long and arduous. Nothing, indeed, is obvious in the story of a ghost. First of all, one has to be born among the living: a thing which is not so much impossible as unreasonable, since life is a scant discontinuity in nothingness, which is eternal and immortal and everywhere. As well, living things must live in time, which does not exist, since it is a form of nothingness. So life must generate time and, so to speak, throw itself into it; until finally—incomprehensible event—after many adventures, it dies. Some hold the belief, but err, that everyone, at death, becomes a ghost. A person who is dead is no longer required to generate time, and must instead abide within a space which is both narrow and infinite. A person who desires to become a ghost must strive to penetrate into still another space, but a space which, even while similar to the one he inhabited while alive, is devoid of time. Few who make the attempt succeed. But those who do come to find themselves in an extremely onerous condition: in fact, they reacquire the use of the objects and, at times, of the persons they knew in life, but this use is entirely mental and abstract, as though these living things were dead and the ghost were alive, but alone and unreachable. So a ghost at times desires to generate a ghost from out of himself, almost a pregnancy, if not for the fact that ghosts have no sex. He must choose within his narrow space the place that generates within him the most uncomfortable suffering; he must recognize the place in which his solitude is intolerable; in which the past transfixes him with inexhaustible rancor; the place where the non-existence of the other is so intense as to constitute a form of existence. He must enter, with his fragile, futile outline, into nothingness, and allow himself to be touched by it, tempted, interrogated, challenged. Though the phrase can make no sense for a ghost, he must suffer a new death. And finally, at times, it very rarely happens that limbs issue from limbs, that a gleam takes flight from a luminescence; and, exhausted, he will have to pursue it; and since they cannot touch each other, he will have to hold it in his company with a perfect balance of indifference and love: and perhaps that place of desolation will hear, unlistened to, a subdued conversation.

FIFTY-FIVE

That gentlemen, correctly dressed in gray, with glasses, slightly academic, who now is crossing the street—to be exact, he is crossing through a bus which has halted at the stoplight—is an hallucination. Since hallucinations have now grown rare and listless, he serves as an hallucination for three people. The first is a gentleman widower who tends toward philosophic introspection, and who at times attempts conversion to one or another religion: attempts generally clumsy and imprecise. With him, the hallucination speaks in elevated words of the World, of Good, of Evil, and, more generically, of God. The second person to whom he offers his services is an attractive and melancholy woman with an imprecise desire for Love and Truth; his task is to persuade her that she not only is worthy of both, but is as well in some way a creditor of the cosmos. With her he makes no mention of God, since she is an extremely earthly person, even if alien to all frivolity or carnality; he makes frequent use of quotations from poets, which he jots down in a pocket notebook and frequently reviews; at times, for her, he must also simulate playing the piano, which in reality is played by a ghost, an unassuming bohemian musician, who has remained without a castle owing to the war. The third case is the most demanding: it's a question, in fact, of an extremely nervous gentleman who is inclined to premonitions, and destined to die in eighteen days in an automobile accident. The relationship here is tempestuous: he cannot address him with the quietude with which he speaks to the man who tends to convert himself, nor with the feeling for poetry with which he caresses the delicate soul of the melancholy woman; he has to insult him, attack him, deride him, since that's what the man who's about to die desires; his temperament, ever since his having been gripped by the premonition of imminent demise, has grown dramatic, and he intently pursues a decisive crisis: he wants to know himself. He is in search of a conversion to himself, and he thinks he'll be able to achieve it only by speaking to himself with extreme brutality, without regard, without affection, hounding himself without reprieve toward the double closure of death and of knowledge of self. The hallucination finds it painful to insult this gentleman, and knows that such brutality will not do the man a great deal of good; but inside himself he feels the anguish, the desperation, the fury of that man who is living his life's last hours. And while deriding him, the hallucination intimately, silently weeps for him.

FIFTY-SIX

That gentleman with the irritable air, and in a general condition of agitation, as though continually challenged by a situation of intolerable gravity, is arguably in love; more exactly, that is how he would describe himself at this particular moment, since it is ten o'clock in the morning and starting at this hour and continuing then till eleven, or at most eleven fifteen, he loves a distinguished woman, of noble spirit, cultivated, slightly authoritarian, silent, and discreetly afflicted. The situation, nonetheless, has this irritating feature: starting at ten fifteen—the lady rises slightly later than the gentleman—and up until eleven thirty, the lady loves a cultivated but brutal student of the Tarot pack, who at the very same hour loves an English matron who has reached her thirtieth lesson in Sanskrit. Around eleven thirty, everything changes. The woman who studies Sanskrit contracts a weakness for the irritable gentleman, who for an hour loves no one at all, even despite an innocuous inclination toward a girl employed as a pillow designer, recently arrived from the countryside, who at just about noon falls in love for forty-five minutes with a young tenor of slight success but fair talent who, in reality, is enamored, up until half past one, of the slightly authoritarian woman. The early afternoon sees a general attenuation of the reciprocal loves, except in the case of the tenor, who cultivates a hopeless veneration for the

lady who studies Sanskrit. At five o'clock in the afternoon, the situation is marked by the introduction
of a middle-aged zoologist, who has finally come to
the realization that life without the simple natural-
ness of the pillow designer is void of meaning; the
zoologist is accompanied by his youthful wife who
thinks, in alternation, to vent her jealousy in the
murder if not of her zoologist husband, then surely
of the pillow designer—though the girl in truth is
unaware even of the zoologist's existence—or who,
lacking that, decides, if the day is Friday or Tuesday,
to love to distraction the brutal adept of the Tarot
pack, who, meanwhile, has written a desperate love
letter to a very young stamp collector, a letter however which he will not send since once again in the
interim he has fallen in love with the slightly authoritarian woman, who has decided to love the irritable
gentleman, who only now has known a foretaste of
cheer, having peered into the eyes of the zoologist's
wife while she instead was making mental vows to a
baritone ruined by the hiccups, unaware of his having decided, after having been rejected by the stamp
collector, to enter a monastery and give up a search
for happiness that did not seem compatible with the
existence of the clock.

FIFTY-SEVEN

In a room located on the fourth floor of a building more solemn than noble, inside a three-room-plus-bath-and-kitchen apartment, a gentleman balding at the temples has today, Sunday, decided to begin to write a book. He has never before written books, and all in all has not even read very many of them, and those in general had been stupid books, or of meager intellectual weight. In truth, there is no moral or practical reason why he ought to write a book; but during the night between Saturday and Sunday, his soul had developed that bizarre outgrowth which includes the idea that writing a book is a noble and ennobling activity. He realizes that he has never in his life done anything noble, which is absolutely exact, but less exceptional than he believes; he has not even carried out the modest social duties which more or less all carry out, such as marrying, supporting a wife and a mistress, fathering a couple of children and sending them decently dressed to school. His relationships have all been cold and absent-minded, since he finds no pleasure in spending money on anything, and all the same is not stingy. He is simply acquainted with nothing that might justify a fatuous and dissipate use of money. He is not religious, but not unreligious either, since both attitudes require an aggressiveness he does not have. He does not read philosophy, which moreover he would not understand. He holds a position as a first-class clerk, which forces him to make no grave decisions, and offers him no exciting prospects, which moreover he would not want, since he finds a boring life to be far more reasonable than an exciting one. All the same, he has decided this Sunday to write a book. He wants to ennoble his life, but clandestinely: the publication of the book will be posthumous. Or perhaps it will not be published, but will be discovered after two hundred years, and he will enjoy all the advantages of glory, without any of the useless dispersals of energy that glory brings with it. There are difficulties. He does not know what a book is; he does not know how long it has to be in order to be a book. More than anything else, he does not know if it has to talk about something or nothing. He has no memoirs to relate, and he would not relate them; shall he write a novel, a divagation, or a meditation? He is perplexed. He feels a vague discomfort. No, it will not talk about love. He has tried the ploy of simply opening the dictionary, but has always come up with words like "dog" or "train." He thinks that someone is insulting him, and urging his retreat; and he looks slowly everywhere around him, grinding his teeth.

FIFTY-EIGHT

For the last several days, he has been extremely on edge; in fact, after a lengthy stretch of living alone, he has realized that the house in which he lives is also inhabited by other beings. In the three rooms of his slightly maniacal apartment, three ghosts, two fairies, one spirit, and a devil have taken up residence; and an enormous angel which alone is as large as a room. He also has the impression that there are other beings, minuscule and spherical, of which he does not know the name. Naturally, the sudden crowd upsets him; he does not understand why these beings have all chosen his house; and he does not understand what purpose they may serve. But nothing disturbs him more than the fact that these beings refuse to let themselves be seen, to speak with him, to converse with him in any way at all, even by signs. He knows he cannot continue to live in such an infested house, but if at least he were able to speak with those images, their mysterious invasion would have a meaning, and perhaps would shed some sort of meaning on his own life. From a simply practical point of view, he can offer no proof of the existence of those beings in his house, and all the same their presence is not only distinct and disquieting, but obvious. He has attempted to induce them to reveal themselves. He addressed the three ghosts, one at a time, and suggested that they might make noises to frighten the building's tenants. Since the silence in no way changed, he turned to the devil, who is notoriously partial, for professional reasons, to dialog. He alluded to the possibility of a business arrangement, and spoke with deliberate nonchalance of his soul, hoping either to blandish the devil, or to irritate the angel. Obtaining no reply, he scattered flowers throughout the room to attract the attention of the fairies; he made use of methods of proven efficacy to call the spirit. But his house, in fact, is crowded with entities that do not want to have anything to do with him. Only the tiny spheres treat him with any courtesy, and he hears from time to time a rapid buzzing at his ears. What he does not know is that the three ghosts, the two fairies, and the spirit are waiting for the next tenant, who will take over the apartment after his imminent death; the angel and the devil are there to attend to the bureaucratic formalities. In a distant province, the future tenant is feverishly packing his bags in order definitively to leave behind a house infested by spirits.

FIFTY-NINE

A gentleman without imag-
ination and enamored of fine cuisine met himself,
the first time, at a bus stop. He recognized himself
immediately, and felt only a bland astonishment; he
knew that, even if rare, such events were possible,
indeed not infrequent. He considered it opportune
to make no show of having recognized himself, since
they had never been introduced. He met himself
the second time along a crowded thoroughfare, and
on the third occasion in front of a store for men's
clothing. This third time, they briefly gave a nod
toward one another, but did not speak. On each occasion he had carefully examined himself. He had
found that himself was distinguished, and elegant,
but burdened with a sad, or a least a thoughtful air
which he could not understand. It was only on their
fifth encounter that they exchanged a subdued "How
do you do?" Indeed, he smiled and noticed, or so at
least it seemed to him, that the other did not return
his smile. The seventh time, at a theater exit, chance
had it that they were pushed towards one another
by the crowd. Himself greeted him cordially, and
made a few comments on the play they had both just
seen—comments which struck him as judicious. He,
in turn, remarked on the actors, and himself agreed
on a number of his points. Starting at the beginning
of any winter, the encounters grew more frequent: it
was clear that he and himself lived in parts of town

which were not far from one another; the fact of their similar habits was hardly to be found surprising. But he grew ever more convinced that himself had an overly despondent air. One evening he went so far as to broach a conversation, beginning with the phrase, "My friend." The talk, affable and courteous, led him to ask if himself didn't have some problem of which he was unaware, even though such a possibility struck him as lying outside the norm. Himself, after brief hesitation, confessed that he was in love, and hopelessly so, with a woman who in any event did not deserve his love; so, no matter if he won her or not, he was damned to a painful, intolerable situation. The gentleman was taken aback by the revelation, since he wasn't in love with any woman. And he trembled at the thought that so great a divide had sprung up between them, so profound as to be thoroughly insurmountable. He attempted to dissuade himself, but himself replied that to love or not to love could be no decision of his own. From that day forward, the gentleman fell into a sullen despondency. He spends most of his time alone with himself, and those who chance to meet him see two distinguished gentlemen in quiet conversation with each other, one of whom, his head concealed in shadow, sometimes assents, sometimes rebuts.

SIXTY

A meticulous but slightly absent-minded gentleman one day received a letter which in fact he had been awaiting for quite some time. The letter came from the Bureau of Existences, and told him, with laconic politeness, that his declaration of existence was imminent, and that therefore he ought to prepare himself to enter existence on short notice. He was happy with the message, and did nothing, since already some time before he had taken all necessary steps to start existing, as of any moment, with or without forewarning. Mildly euphoric at the thought of existing, he looked upon that moment in which he currently found himself, that breach between existing and non-existing, as a sort of vacation. Since nothing could happen to him for as long as he had not begun truly to exist, he treated himself with a certain generosity: he got up late, walked for most of the day, made brief trips to restful and picturesque places. He awaited the definitive communication, without impatience, since he knew that the procedures were delicate, the operations subtle, the distances enormous, the mails inefficient. Three months after the first letter, he received a second, which informed him of an error: the previous letter had been delivered to him on account of a diachronic homonomy, since a man with his very same name and surname would be born in six centuries time, in that same city. Accordingly, the previous letter had been annulled, and his file had been reopened, and would be clarified; though the letter made no mention of an imminent existence, its tone was encouraging. He felt a mild disappointment, but couldn't presume he had anything to feel bad about, since, after all, he was a very small thing in the universe. So he attempted to see the postponement as a further vacation; but he could not deny a touch of something bitter in his innocent amusements. The third letter arrived after another six months; clearly it had nothing to do with him, someone must have sent him a letter intended for someone else, since here there was talk of a death of his as having already taken place, and complaint was made of a neglected return of the left shoulder to the quartermaster. He could not avoid the thought that there were grave shortcomings at the Bureau of Existences, and he regretted it. After a year, a new letter, bizarrely ungrammatical, referred again to the question of the left shoulder, and bore a date nine centuries later than the day on which it arrived. Carefully examining the envelope, he noted a slight inaccuracy in the way his name was written, and he ceased in precisely that instant both to pre-exist and to non-exist.

SIXTY-ONE

A young man is on his way to a rendezvous with a young woman, to whom he intends to say that he finds it useless, harmful, wasteful and monotonous that they continue to see each other. In reality, he has never loved this young woman, but felt for her a sequence of feelings of gallantry, devotion, admiration, hope, perplexity, detachment, disappointment, irritation. Irritation is now quietly slipping over into a form of bland and demeaning pique, since he supposes that the woman is in some way unwilling to forget him, and he fears that within her life he has assumed a dignity which he finds alarming. Reviewing the series of feelings he has felt for the young woman, he recognizes that at times he behaved with excessive fragility, and had hoped…had hoped what? He had hoped that both of them were different, and that they had possessed a space in which to invent a relationship; he admits that a part of his dilemma doesn't depend on her, but on his own behavior, laughably fantastic and irresponsible.

At the very same moment, the young woman is making her way to the rendezvous, firmly intending to make everything clear. She is a woman with a love for simplicity and clarity, and she feels that the imprecisions and ambiguities of a non-existent relationship have gone on too long. She never loved that man, but must admit to having been weak; to a lack of caution in the way she had asked for his aid; to having tolerated the growth of a tacit misunderstanding in which now she feels herself unfairly trapped. The woman is irritated, but prudence advises that she only be decided and calm. She knows that this man is a creature of emotion, a fantasizer, capable of seeing things that are not there, and of trusting in such things with a faith no less constant than empty and unfounded; she also knows this man to have a high opinion of himself, and to be inclined to lie simply to prevent it from suffering humiliation. So, she will be prudent, benevolent, clear-headed.

Punctually, the young man and woman approach their appointed meeting place. Now they have seen each other, have greeted one another, with a gesture in which habit has replaced cordiality. Having reached a distance of only a couple of yards from one another, each halts to survey the other, attentively, in silence; and both are suddenly overwhelmed by a fury of joy, as both understand, and know, that neither of them has ever loved the other.

SIXTY-TWO

*E*xiting a shop into which
he had entered to purchase an aftershave lotion, a
middle-aged gentleman, well-mannered and serious, saw that they had robbed him of the Universe.
In place of the Universe, there was only a grayish
dust, the city had disappeared, the sun was gone, no
sound came out of that dust, which apparently was
entirely accustomed to its métier as dust. Of calm
disposition, the gentleman found no cause to make a
scene; a theft had taken place, a larger than ordinary
theft, but a theft nonetheless. The gentleman was in
fact convinced that someone had stolen the Universe
under cover of the moment in which he had entered
the store. Not that the Universe belonged to him, but
having been born, and being alive, he had a certain
right to the use of it. On entering the store, he in fact
had left the Universe outside, without the precaution
of securing it with lock and chain, which indeed he
never used, owing to the enormous dimensions that
made its use impractical. Despite his severity with
himself, he did not feel guilty of insufficient vigi-
lance, or any lack of caution. He knew that he lived
in a city afflicted by an insolent underworld, but no
theft of the Universe had ever taken place. The calm
gentleman turned around, and, as he expected, the
shop too had disappeared. So, it was not unlikely that
the thieves were still not too far away. All the same,
he felt impotent and somewhat irritated; a thief who

pilfers everything, including all police stations and all officers on the beat, is a thief who moves into a privileged position which thieves as a rule do not enjoy. Even while remaining calm, the gentleman felt that state of mind which often has prompted other gentlemen to write letters to the directors of newspapers; and had there been any newspapers, he perhaps would have done just that. In the same way, had there been a police station, he would have filed a complaint, specifically stating that the Universe did not belong to him, but that he used it every day, and had done so since his birth, in a sober and attentive manner, without his ever having been called to account by the authorities. But the police stations were all gone, and the gentleman felt embarrassed, derided, abused. He was asking himself whatever he ought to do, when, unmistakably, someone touched him on the shoulder, softly, to call him.

SIXTY-THREE

*A*n illustrious bell-caster, with a long beard and unconditionally an atheist, one day received a visit from two clients. They were dressed in black, and very serious, and showed a swelling on their shoulders, which made it cross the atheist's mind that that was where their wings might be, as are said to be found on angels; but he paid this thought no attention, since it didn't align with his convictions. The two gentlemen commissioned a bell of great dimensions—the master had never before made anything similar—and they wanted it cast in an alloy he had never before employed. They explained that the bell would emit a special sound, utterly different from the sound of any other bell. At the moment of departing, the two gentlemen explained, not without a trace of embarrassment, that the bell was to serve for Judgment Day, which by now was imminent. The master bell-maker laughed a friendly laugh, and said that there would never be a Judgment Day, but that all the same he would make the bell as indicated, and within the established time. The two gentlemen paid him a visit every two or three weeks to see how the work was proceeding. They were two gloomy gentlemen, and, despite their admiration for the master's work, seemed secretly dissatisfied. Then, for a time, they didn't return. Meanwhile, the master bell-caster had brought to completion the largest bell of his life, and recognized that he was proud of it; and in the secret place of his dreams he could see himself desire that so beautiful a bell, unique throughout the world, be used on the occasion of Judgment Day. When the bell had been finished, and mounted on a great wooden trestle, the two gentlemen reappeared; they looked upon the bell with admiration, and at the very same time with profound despondency. They sighed. Finally, the one who seemed more authoritative turned to the bell-caster and confessed in a low voice, "You were right, dear master; there will not be, neither now nor ever, any Judgment Day. There has been a terrible mistake." The master bell-maker regarded the two gentlemen, he too with a melancholy air, but his melancholy was happy and benevolent. "I'm afraid it's too late, gentlemen," he said with a quiet, steady voice. He pulled the cord, and the great bell swung and sounded, loud and strong, and, as it had to be, the Heavens opened.

SIXTY-FOUR

The young man who is waiting for the stoplight to consent to his crossing the street is on his way to the home of a woman to whom he intends somehow to declare himself, hoping to be rejected. He is very good at being told "no," and at living in general in an atmosphere of continuous rejection. On the few occasions when he has been accepted, he has only managed to stir up a terrible confusion, and as a rule he ceases to want to see a woman who has voiced a "yes." In truth, he is not even in love with the woman to whom he intends somehow to make a declaration, but he supposes that she expects it, and he cannot disobey the will, even if rigorously implicit, of a woman whom he cannot deny admiring. Were he less disinclined to a "yes," the young man might even be able to love this woman, in the frank and virile manner he supposes natural to him, even if this frank and virile manner is something he has never had the chance to test. But in truth, and not unwisely—being convinced that the result of his declaration will in any case be a "no," and that the woman indeed demands his declaration in order to be able to exercise her right of refusal, and it also being clear to him that such a "no" is what he himself desires, in satisfaction of both the woman's will and his own most intimate calling—he has avoided falling in love, so as not to color the situation in too explicitly naturalistic and painful tones. Everything will in any case be painful, that much is clear, given his talent for painfulness, but with time he has learned to moderate his hunger for degradation, and it's enough for him to feel himself generically cast aside. He has the impression of having chosen the right woman: meek, kind, a little set off from life, pretty but afraid she isn't, surely she'll reject him with tact, she'll say that she feels flattered, or she'll say something noble and elevated, she'll talk about friendship, or perhaps confess to him that her heart belongs to another; in short, she will not render his duty intolerable, his duty to make her a declaration, since, after all, he is doing so primarily to please her. He hopes with all his heart that he has not tripped into a painful misunderstanding, since experience has taught him that a "yes" is simply and only a remanded "no," a double "no," a two-tiered "no" with none of the painful and delicate comforts of a "no." Full of confidence, he now crosses the street, as though directing himself to a new life.

SIXTY-FIVE

The knight who has slain the dragon—a fine figure of a man, of splendid bearing, slender and clean, even though mortal—ties the great mass of fearsome meat to his saddle, and sets out on the road toward the city. He is proud of his achievement, even though he darkly realizes that his spear was guided by equal parts of destiny and stupidity. He makes his way through villages, and the people, habitually in terror of the monster, close themselves up in their homes and bolt the doors. The knight laughs, and thinks that in the city the king will embrace him in the sight of the whole of the populace, and, at least for good form, will offer him his daughter's hand in marriage. The knight, dragging along the body, the teeth, the half-closed eyes of the dragon, passes next to a cemetery, a church, a lonely house. But no one peers out to pay him homage: not even the dead, who restrict themselves to a murmur which might also hold reprobation; why doesn't the priest come out to bless the dragon slayer? Why don't the people who live in the house come out to kiss his stirrups? Are they perhaps afraid of him, of the man who has freed them from the monstrous monster? The knight is annoyed, and all the more proud of his feat. He passes now through the city gates, proceeds along the great road that leads to the palace; the street is crowded, but as he advances he feels that something strange is taking place: the people fall silent, draw back, avert their eyes, and he knows they do not do so to avoid the sight of the horrible monster, but so as not to look at him, the knight. He cannot avoid the awareness of being met with a sense of repugnance. It's not that the people of the city are afraid of him; it's rather that he turns their stomachs. The knight is appalled, indignant, bewildered. A window slams sharply shut, he hears or thinks he hears a rapid volley of insults. But didn't he slay the dragon? Hadn't they all agreed that the dragon had to be slain? Wasn't history laden with stories of paladins who slaughtered dragons, and found themselves rewarded with women and palaces and Japanese motorcycles? Had he perhaps mixed up dragons and killed the wrong one? No, no one had ever talked about two dragons, there are never two dragons, not in any case. He would like to feel angry, but instead he feels forlorn; he doesn't understand. He sees that it's not a good idea to pay a visit to the king, and he reins in his horse at a cross-roads, where people melt back away from him. What shall he do? The knight descends from his steed, and turns to look at the dragon, ugly and motionless. For the first time, he studies its body, its face, its hard skin, its extended claws; what feelings does he experience, the knight? For the first time he feels dismay, and sees his fate as a dragon killer to be risible and depraved; and he realizes, confusedly, that he will live out the rest of his life in contemplation of that incorruptible corpse.

SIXTY-SIX

A fairy from the land of the fairies, known for her absent-mindedness, and also for an irritating uselessness that marked her undertakings, one day boarded the wrong train, and instead of reaching a country where other fairies lived to whom she was related, all of them slightly fatuous, she arrived in a land where no fairies lived at all, and never had. The fairy grasped her situation only after leaving the train, and realized as well that she didn't have the slightest idea where she was. For a while she wandered here and there hoping to meet another fairy; but before too long she was forced to realize that this was fairyless territory. The hapless creature felt adrift, and was greatly chagrined. She had no idea what train she had taken instead of the proper one, and therefore had no way to trace her trip backwards. She decided to turn to a slightly un-dignified expedient, and to choose a person to whom to make herself visible. Children would have been a good solution from certain points of view, but would not have been able to supply the information she needed. The elderly, too, would have done, but she was afraid of their chattering tongues, their craving to make themselves indiscriminately useful. Finally she chose a gentleman with an air both calm and ex-cessively thoughtful. This man, in fact, was slightly inclined to hallucinations, paranoid fantasies, cre-puscular states of mind: in short, his controlling notion of the world was extremely realistic and well articulated. He believed in fairies, in magical numbers, in the Flying Dutchman. When the fairy materialized in front of him, he responded with a suitable greeting, and expressed with sober eloquence the pleasure of meeting so distinguished a fairy. In spite of being a man of slight account, might he be of help to her? Yes, she replied, he could. That made him happy. The fairy explained her situation, and the excessively thoughtful gentleman courteously escorted her to the station, put her on the right train, explained at what station she ought to get off, and took leave of her with a bow. His eyes were full of tears as he walked away, since he realized that in that instant the whole of his life had been explained, and that the explanation would never be repeated. The fairy felt kindly toward the thoughtful gentleman, and thought it would be polite to return and pay him a visit. Then she forgot about him. The thoughtful gentleman never forgot the fairy; every now and then he goes to the station to see that train; every now and then he boards it, and travels for two or three stations. Then he gets off, reboards the train in the other direction, and attempts to hold firmly in his slender hands that minimal meaning, but a total meaning, which had come to him through the grace of an absent-minded fairy: to him, a dull and distracted man, and to no one else in the city.

SIXTY-SEVEN

The animal pursued by the hunters undergoes, in the course of its silent and meticulous flight, a series of transformations which make it impossible to give of it a credible scientific description. In the first part of its flight, it bears resemblance to the fox, with red fur, but a longer snout than adopted by the fox or any of the felines; it has a long and restless tail, and by moving it back and forth it cancels out its footprints. All the same, the dogs but rarely allow themselves to be thrown off track by this facile deception, and the beast therefore begins to alter its form and color. At times it turns green, so as to camouflage and hide itself in the thick of the forest, and possesses erect quills, which hold at bay its assailants; it has laid aside its tail, and runs by way of great leaps, with sudden shifts of direction. For as long as it holds this form, the hunters may attempt to strike it with slings and stones, since until it further shifts its aspect there is nothing else they can do. Stones rarely harm it: but if their threat grows real, we see the creature now lengthen out into a kind of winged, bluish snake which slithers smooth and moist through the grasses and among the rocks; it hisses, and a thin vapor issues from its mouth; its eyes are yellow. The hunters can shoot arrows at the winged snake; but even when well-aimed, they do not sink into its flesh, but only glancingly wound its skin, shedding no blood. Even though winged, the snake does not fly, or flies only very close to the ground; and if a hunter were able, with a swift horse, to overtake and run before it, and to fire an arrow backward into its mouth, the beast would be killed. But horses so fast are rare, and generally of mild disposition. At this point, the beast still possesses the possibility of a definitive mutation; formerly lengthened out, it now proceeds to flatten into a disc, like certain fish, and in a moment the distance between its rear and its face has shrunk to a few centimeters. At this point it is a vast animal, nearly a broad, thin moon: an easy target, and the hunter can fire at it with a gun, without missing; but its substance is so diffuse that bullets traverse it while never, or almost never, wounding it. But the hunter has little time: the monster, in fact, without turning around, suddenly inverts its face and rear, and dogs and horses and hunters find themselves confronted by an enormous toothed mouth, which, mute and thrown wide open, assails, slashes, lacerates and devours them.

SIXTY-EIGHT

Whenever he anchors in a port, the captain of the Flying Dutchman goes ashore with his first mate; he always has a great deal of money with him, in the coin that's current in the port in which he's landed; the money is brought to him, alternately, by a demon and an angel. The captain, like an old salt happy to find himself again in a warm and populated place, enters a tavern and greets all present with great cordial waves of the hand, and with ceremonious burlesque bows. The first mate—a tall, thin and pallid man—limits himself to the taciturn smile of a subordinate. But the captain is always in his finest spirits; there he is as he offers rounds of drink, and demands that he and his guests be served the best the house can offer; and he pays for it all with that money of his which is always new, and makes so strange a ring on the inn-keeper's counter. The captain makes no mystery of himself: he immediately presents himself, in a robust voice, as the captain of the Flying Dutchman. His declaration is met by some with cordial laughs, like a daring jest one's amused to hear on the lips of others, though no one else in the tavern would be bold enough to pronounce it. But others find it disturbing, and there is always someone who abandons the company with a certain haste. It's a great shame, since the captain always has a stock of fine and spicy stories to tell, while his pallid mate, a bit too pallid, listens without joining in. The captain tells stories of pirates, of buried treasures that all search for and no one finds; and also stories of stunningly beautiful women, for the winning of whom no escapade at all could be more than a bagatelle; and then duels; and where good wine is found; and the whales that swim the oceans with a forest on their back, those forests where the sirens live. He also tells stories of pranks, of deceptions, of feminine wiles; and his language, one has to admit, is not always as temperate as is ought to be. But his listeners aren't people who take offense. Finally he takes his leave, again with bows and waves of the hand as he backs away toward the door; then he turns, opens the door to make his exit, and is met by the first gust of wind in the streets. The assembled company now looks on, at first incredulous, then horrified, as the captain's clothes and those of his mate go limp and crumple up, as though they had no bodies, indeed as though their clothes were entirely empty. As the two fluttering suits move off into the distance, the gathering, grown silent, thinks back to the captain's tales and understands that he lied, and that no one will ever hear him tell the torturous stories of his navigations, the things which have really been seen by those nonexistent eyes.

SIXTY-NINE

The astrologer—a man with a quiet and in no way fanciful aspect—has just finished his calculations, and surveys them with a touch of bitter amusement. These calculations, performed and checked with care, reveal the following: he will meet the woman of his life in one year and six months; in many ways she presents herself as a woman of destiny, and demands nothing more than to be accepted. The astrologer has no objection, being a man obedient to the needs of the cosmos, and those needs include this encounter with a woman who for him is a fate. But his calculations have also told him something else: specifically, that he will die exactly twenty days prior to the meeting with his woman. The astrologer has a certain sense of humor, and cannot withhold a smile; this is truly a riddle. On the day of the meeting the woman will undoubtedly be alive; and he, no less undoubtedly, dead; all the same, the underlying order of the cosmos as a whole appears to be so inflexible, that the meeting cannot not take place. The astrologer reflects: is it perhaps that his ghost will fall in love with the woman to whom he is destined, and reveal itself to her? It is not impossible, in theory, but this would make it the very first case of a prophecy concerned with the life of a ghost, with the sentimental education of a dead man. As well, what sort of relationship might arise between himself dead and her alive? It is equally beside the point to consider reincarnation, since in even the event, technically improbable, of an instantaneous reincarnation, he, on that day, would be twenty days old. He fantasizes: the woman might fall in love with his portrait, but can a portrait be what is meant by "he"? So, if any sort of solution is possible, it must have to do with a rule of the world which no one until now has fathomed or grazed against: a rule, as in the case he himself has discovered, which foresees a thing he finds it hard to define. Perhaps it's the impossible, perhaps it's error. If in fact it's the impossible, it means that the universe holds within itself the need for something which cannot be, and thus is in conflict with itself; and, in all likelihood, taken as a whole, that the universe is unhappy. If the rule foresees and imposes error, it means that the world has reached a point at which only imprecision can reveal it to itself, where only mendacity can tell it the truth, sickness heal it, death create it. If this is the case, the day of his meeting with his woman would be the last day of a Great Year, the day on which the world is to burn and rebegin.

SEVENTY

The young man, pensive and dispirited, who sits on a park bench in a secluded and solitary place indeed has excellent cause to be pensive, dispirited, and in seclusion. He finds himself, in fact, in the onerous condition of being in love with three women; and this alone would already be excessive and extravagant. It must be added, however—though strictly speaking he cannot be said to know it—that two of these three women lived one and three centuries before his birth, and that the third will be born two centuries after his death. So, even while absolutely and pitifully in love, he has never met any of these women, nor ever will be able to. And despite not knowing it with certainty, he is aware that his enamorment is quite bizarre, and can lead to nothing good. First of all, one cannot marry three women, and even courting them is difficult. Moreover, how can he say he is in love if he has never seen them, has never been in the company of any of the three in even the most innocent way? Finally, he cannot remain unaware of the feeling that his never having met them is no chance matter and, equally, derives from no spiteful or hostile resolve on the ladies' part: that it possesses instead an intrinsic necessity of its own, involved, basically, with the very reason why he loves them. There are three of them, so they reciprocally cancel each other out; they have never been seen, so he has no knowledge of what he loves; and thanks to their definitive invisibility, he will never be able to fall out of love. Because this is the most dramatic point: he has no way to experience a colloquy with any of these three women, nor even to taste their presence in the world of life; he cannot anticipate encounters, plan rendezvous, fantasize intimacies; he has no way even of knowing where to try to find them, and this is why he cannot free his mind from this devastating condition of being perennially in love, with whom or what he himself is unable to say, but indubitably in love. At the very same time, he experiences an extravagant respect for his condition, as though what has befallen him, absurd and impossible, were a symptom of something far more luminous than himself; as though he had been touched by a miracle, or marked with a predestination; but then, with a sigh, crossing his legs and closing his eyes, he imagines himself to be a sore, a wart, a malformation of the park, of the city, of the world, or perhaps a single and entirely untranslatable hieroglyphic.

SEVENTY-ONE

The man is at the center of the city. The great white square is delimited by very tall buildings, so tall that one cannot see their summits. The light is a delicate twilight, whether about to collapse into night, or proceed toward day, we do not know. The city is deserted. He knows that in the bright white houses, in the rectilinear streets, in the geometric squares, there is neither man nor animal. He is the center of the city, its meaning, its map. He cannot tell if he is in that place as sovereign, as martyr, or as forgotten prisoner. For what he knows of himself, he might even be a monument, simply the city's most privileged place. His notions concerning himself are indistinct, but everything he remembers is in some way connected with the city, even though not only he, but no one at all, as far as he knows, has ever lived there, been born there, died there. He knows there is a reason why he, *par excellence*, is the city's inhabitant: and it lies in the atrocious, sovereign suffering those straight lines inflict upon him, in that cruel pallor. Immobile at the center of the city, he feels the whole of it, mapped out in his anguish. For quite some time, he has contemplated flight; but flight would mean to relinquish suffering, and his suffering is what makes him not only the center, but the monarch of the empty city. Yet he also knows that because he is its monarch he ought to flee, giving death to the city that exclusively exists in the pride it feels for its center, monument, suffering, explanation and king. Everything has been constructed in the conviction, in the certain prophecy that he will never leave that place, that he will never attempt to reach the gates, all wide open, that offer passage through its walls. So, all of this repeats to him that his flight is necessary, that he must lose meaning to acquire meaning, he must abdicate to become king. To be the city's meaning is at once to be its victim and executioner. In the moment when the project of flight grows lucid and intolerable, he becomes aware of the city's suffering, of the panic of its towering buildings. He sees that he detests this proud and cowardly city, and in every part of his body he measures the power of life and death that he, as monarch, exercises over the whole of it. Immobile, he decides to flee, to kill, to turn the city, his pride, into a bleached expanse of indecipherable ruins.

SEVENTY-TWO

His métier is as the Dream-
stuff; it is a profession he likes, since it allows him
not to have a constant form, and to fluctuate among
all the possible forms that can be of use in a dream,
with one limitation: he is the Maleficent Dreamstuff,
which means that his employment is in all the evil
roles, from the fascist to the witch. He has a liking
for the animal forms: he's good as the snake, as a
rabid dog; at times they have him do Cerberus, or
Herod, and Herod particularly suits him, what with
the regal cape and all the servants. He also likes his
job because he knows that his interventions, no matter how distressing, are welcomed by the dreamers.
In general, a dream that sees the appearance of the
Maleficent Dreamstuff has a certain dignity, and can
also contain great meanings. Even though, taken
alone, the Maleficent Dreamstuff implies no great
illuminations, he's pleased to be in the vicinity of
revelations, of profound discoveries on the part of
the soul, though of course he does not like the soul.
The Maleficent Dreamstuff, in spite of knowing how
to be extremely unpleasant, is not the Nightmare.
With a specialized course he might become a Nightmare, but the profession of Nightmare is doubtless
much more onerous, even if appearances are less
frequently called for. He has a number of friends
among the Nightmares, and is proud of it, just as
he is proud of being permitted to dine from time to

time at the table of the Meanings, which in general are shy and fussy. Spending time with the Meanings is highly agreeable, since it's rare and flattering to be taken into their confidence; but the Nightmares are often depressing, and the way they laugh is not relaxing. Moreover, Nightmares are not popular among dreamers, but only among men of letters, who ask to be told them by people who don't know how to write. Painters, too, love the Nightmares. Nightmares, unlike the Maleficent Dreamstuff, are not obliged to take on form, and can be pure indeterminacy. Mostly, however, when they entertain guests, they take on the guise of horses, or of dummies. In any case, the Dreamstuff does not hesitate to frequent them, since their friendship is a source of social distinction. Moreover, despite their being a wholly different thing, one can always learn a couple of points of professional finesse. When all is said and done, the Dreamstuff has something of the parvenu, but he's never short of work and his standard of living is quite respectable. Moreover, it's customarily up to him, and not to the Nightmares, to announce catastrophes and death, which is a calling that's generally held to be not without distinction.

SEVENTY-THREE

The cry was suddenly heard throughout the village, and as far as one could understand, it was heard with equal intensity at every point, even in the outlying farmhouses. It was also heard, distinctly, by a near deaf carpenter; it was heard by a foreigner who was passing by on a bicycle, and who stopped with his blood running cold. The cry was later described by those who had heard it: all agreed on the fact that it expressed profound desolation, perhaps desperation, and that it might be the cry of someone in imminent danger of death, perhaps menaced by a cruel assassin. All were amazed at the force of the cry, and by the feeling that all had heard it with particular clarity. Some suggested that it hadn't been a question of a single cry, but of multiple cries, from various directions, simultaneously. When the moment of anguish had somewhat subsided, a number of the villagers set themselves to searching throughout the town, and a sort of assembly was mustered in the church, to ascertain who might be missing. But no one was missing, except for a student who resided by now in the city, and an old man who two or three days before had entered the hospital of a neighboring town. Some spoke of ghosts, of trolls, of beasts; but this was not a land of beasts; and trolls and ghosts were no longer accepted, not even on the part of the children. The townsmen searched through all the abandoned houses, the solitary retreats; they sent out the dogs, which gave no sign of discomfort. Some of the people went out into the countryside, shook the bushes, examined the bottom of a modest stream. In the late afternoon, the excitement began to abate; the men returned and confirmed they had found no trace of anything out of the ordinary, and no sign of unnatural events. A vague disquiet remained, but toward evening the children returned to playing in the streets. Groups of villagers patrolled the hamlet's streets, but then tired of it and went home. The six couples officially betrothed met with tender apprehension. Dinner was calm, and the evening that followed was warm and serene. Gradually, the cry had become a terrible memory, but a memory which no longer could be relived. Terrible? Perhaps no more than a perfectly natural curiosity: many had already forgotten that that cry had had a voice. At the beginning of night, lights were extinguished, windows closed. No one at that moment knew that in the heart of the night, at exactly two fifteen, the cry would repeat itself.

SEVENTY-FOUR

This calm and properly
educated gentleman was making his way down a quiet, tree-lined street when he heard a sudden drone at
his side, as though of something rolling. He turned
around for a look and saw a funnel-shaped chasm
open up in the earth. The chasm rotated, and grew
wider, until reaching a width of perhaps two meters;
and it continued to rotate. The gentleman, who was
not without a spirit of observation, noted that the
chasm was not stationary; instead, albeit the circumstance seemed implausible, it moved. More exactly,
it accompanied him. He took a few steps, and the
chasm moved along with him, offering him, as it
were, its left, so the calm gentleman thought that it
must be a female chasm. But then came the moment
when the chasm placed itself before him, almost as
though to pitch him into its depths, and he had to
halt. In truth, he was not sure that the abyss intended
to suck him down and do away with him, but surely
it was fond of giving him a sense of insecurity and
imminent peril. The properly educated gentleman
had heard tell of Guardian Chasms which in ancient
times accompanied the monks in the deserts, afford-
ing them the feelings both of being escorted and
molested. He did not know if Guardian Chasms still
existed; this was perhaps an example of such a thing,
though he did not know if vestigial, or premonitory
of the Chasms' rebirth. He proceeded with caution,

but initially without fear; he began to grow nervous when the Chasm moved over to his left, then grazed his heels, abruptly distanced, returned in his direction, and halted a centimeter away from his feet. The gentleman was now less calm, but a certain curiosity had asserted itself within him. So, he turned to the Chasm, and respectfully asked if it had been sent by God. The Chasm appeared surprised at being addressed, and the gentleman received the impression that it blushed. Perhaps, reflected the gentleman, I have behaved impolitely, but I can say that any such thing is only and wholly the Chasm's fault. He felt this Chasm to be somewhat frivolous. He asked it, not without a touch of insolence, if they had already met, if they had reason to think themselves entitled to a certain intimacy. After a brief hesitation, the Chasm nodded no, not without grace. The gentleman at that point advanced directly toward the Chasm, which withdrew, stood off to one side, and directed a thoughtful glance at the gentleman. The gentleman resumed his path, and on realizing that the Chasm had given up following, he felt an acute, senile sadness.

SEVENTY-FIVE

A *woman has given birth* to a sphere: it's a question of a globe some twenty centimeters in diameter. Delivery was easy, without complications. Whether or not the woman is married is unknown. A husband would have presumed a relationship with the devil, and would have thrown her out of the house, or perhaps would have beaten her to death with a hammer. So, she has no husband. She is said to be a virgin. In any case, she is a good mother: she is very attached to the sphere. Since the sphere has no mouth, she feeds it by immersing it in a small basin filled with her milk. The basin is decorated with flowers. The sphere is perfectly smooth and uninterrupted. It has no eyes, nor any limbs by way of which to move itself, but all the same it rolls about the room, goes up the stairs, bouncing lightly and very gracefully. The material of which it's made is more rigid than flesh, but not completely inelastic. Its movements show will and decision, something that might be referred to as clear ideas. Its mother washes it every day, and feeds it. In reality, it is never dirty. It seems it does not sleep, even though it never disturbs its mother: it emits no sounds. All the same, she believes herself to understand that, in certain moments, the sphere is anxious for her touch; it seems to her that in those moments its surface is softer. People avoid the woman who gave birth to a sphere, but the woman does not notice it. All day long, all night long, her life revolves around the sphere's pathetic perfection. She knows the sphere, no matter how much a prodigy, to be extremely young. She watches it slowly grow. After three months, its diameter has increased by nearly five centimeters. At times its surface, generally gray, takes on a pinkish hue. The mother has nothing to teach the sphere, but tries to learn from it; she follows its movements, attempts to understand if there's something it's "trying to tell her." She has the impression that, no, the sphere has nothing to tell her, but all the same is a part of her. The mother knows the sphere will not remain forever in her home; but this precisely is what touches her: to have been involved in a story both alarming and utterly tranquil. When the days are warm and sunny, she takes the sphere in her arms and goes for a walk outside, around the house. At times she goes as far as a public park, and has the impression that people are getting used to her, to her sphere. She likes to let it roll among the flower beds, to follow it and catch it, with a gesture of fright and passion. The mother loves the sphere, and wonders if ever a woman has been so much a mother as she.

SEVENTY-SIX

The house at the corner of the street is where the Assassin lives. The Thief lives directly across from him, a bit further on is the Lover, and down at precisely the end of the street there lives, alone, the Queen. It's a dark day, and the sun has no desire to make its way into this street. It is in fact a truly miserable street. The Assassin is an easygoing man, and would even be friendly and benevolent, if he had not found his lot in that profession, which, moreover, is a profession he loves. Of course, he has never killed anyone, but his day is entirely given over to the planning of ferocious homicides, and in his home he has built a collection of arms of every type, which he does not know how to handle. In consideration of all of this, he receives a modest pension, addressed to Mr. Assassin. His condition of Assassin permits him a number of experiences which otherwise would be precluded to him: feelings of guilt, fear of being discovered, the need to cover all his traces, repentance, and hope of finally mending his ways. He goes out only at night, when he is sure the streets are empty; he loves rainy nights. For survival, he relies on the courtesy of the Thief, who has never stolen anything, but who is ready to perform whatever chores the Assassin suggests to him. The Thief is thin, delicate, withdrawn, silent. He can walk up to behind a cat without the cat's having realized it. His hands are precise, elegant, and efficient;

but he will never steal anything; he loves that combination of pride and insecurity which is a thief's stock-in-trade. He is always ready for flight, but as proud and courageous as a knight. He knows how to lie, but doesn't lie. He knows how to open every lock, but a door left ajar will stop him. All the same, no one will ever be able to rob him of the happiness of being a thief. The Lover loves, but has no woman to love. So he sighs, writes delicate verses which he reads to the Thief, who has an ear for rhythm. He has readied a beautiful wedding gown, which slowly molders in the closet. He purchases flowers every day, and lets them wither. He is unhappy, and delighted at being so. On occasion the Thief, the Assassin and the Lover meet at the board of a sober, evening meal and speak of the Queen. All of them hold the Queen in great respect, none of them has ever seen her. They think of her invisibility as a sign of great nobility, and the Assassin considers himself her Army, the Thief her Minister, the Lover her Prince Consort. At times they suspect that the Queen is dead, which is even more noble, or that she never existed, which is perfect nobility. But at that point, they all three feel useless, and fall into silence.

SEVENTY-SEVEN

In this city, everyone pos-
sesses something which is indispensable to someone
else, without the possessor knowing what to do with
it, or even knowing they possess it. All are aware of
the lack of something entirely indispensable, but
no one knows who has it, or if the person who has
it knows they have it, or, in case they do know, if
they might be willing to part with it. It also never
happens, so far as anyone knows, that each of two
persons possesses what's indispensable to the other,
which would make, if indeed they recognized each
other, for a fairly easy situation, reducible to an act
of symmetrical exchange. So, the person in possession of something indispensable to someone else
will find no advantage in giving it up unless this
someone else is capable of finding what in turn is
indispensable to the other. It follows that whoever
truly desires what's indispensable to him or her must
not so much, or must not only, search out the party
in possession of what they find indispensable, but
must also, or first of all, seek out the individual presumed to possess what's indispensable to the party
in possession of what's indispensable to themselves.
As a result, the city has seen the creation of a system
of supplication, inquiry, research, investigation, and
begging in which everyone is involved, but indirectly.
It is legitimate to ask how a supplicant can expect
to know what's indispensable to the individual who

holds what's indispensable to the supplicant himself. In truth, there are no sure rules, but little by little there has taken shape a method of divination, or deduction, that approximately follows a course as follows: something is indispensable to me, but is not indispensable to the person in possession of it; now, if what is indispensable to me is useless to him, this means that he must be in need of something that's external to what's indispensable to me, and external as well to everything I possess, but in some way contiguous with both. So, some believe themselves to be able through a process of self-analysis to perceive what it is, at least approximately, that's indispensable to the other. But at this point, it's necessary to discover the person who possesses that indispensable thing, and who in turn would find it advantageous to give it up only if he in turn is furnished with what's indispensable to him. The problem would seem to be insoluble, but since it's a question of indispensable things, no one can abandon the search for solutions, and the search for the indispensable thing becomes finally in its own right indispensable, and it isn't entirely clear whether, in this city, one desires that it come to an end.

SEVENTY-EIGHT

The thoughtful man in the
empty square is plagued by a question both vague
and disquieting. He has the feeling of having omit-
ted some gesture, a choice, a fidelity to principles
which, furthermore, he has never openly espoused;
or simply of having left some letter without a reply;
or of having not foiled a crime to which, *de facto*, he
is now an accomplice. Or perhaps he didn't study the
language which would have opened the road to the
most important books of his life; or he had failed
to keep faith with a promise that he's able neither
to remember nor forget; or he had not made some
obvious, banal gesture which absolutely everyone
demanded nonetheless that he make. So, this man is
even unable to speculate as to whether whatever he
did not do—even while knowing it obscurely to link
with his torment—was an act extended in time, or
virtually instantaneous, a thing of great moment, or
a minimal and unimportant gesture, but of absolute
and intrinsic dignity, by virtue of being entwined
with his destiny. He is certain of having performed
no act that now torments him with its haunting,
indelible presence; he is certain that his great unhappiness derives from an omission which remains
unmentioned and unforgiven. It is likely that that
omission irreparably altered the story of his life,
and that now what once was a dramatic but reasonable destiny spreads out like a shapeless sign, a heap

of rags and refuse. By way of that omission, he has stripped all meaning from an arduous concatenation of events; he has undone his own history, and there is now no force in the world that might restore rectilinear meaning to that itinerary. If he were able to remember the omission, he would certainly attempt to amend it; but it cannot be excluded that the omission might refer to some event, or word, or gesture from a great deal of time before, to something that by now has consumed to the dregs the horror of its absence, and inflicted harm which by now is definitive. In such a case, the lack of meaning in the life he lives would be irrevocable, and he can do nothing other than continue to suffer for that unknown and irreparable omission. Slowly, the man sets out: he now will make his way to the home of the Torturer. In subjecting himself to torture, he hopes that, broken by pain, he'll confess to himself the omission which has worn away the mediocre fabric of his life.

SEVENTY-NINE

The sovereign who con-
demned him, for a crime indicted in a highly imprecise but also threatening way, has had him confined
in a thoroughly decorous residence, with drapes and
musicians, and jars of delicate wines and jams that
stand in vitrines of exquisite facture and fantasti-
cal design. The prisoner reads rare books which
are housed in a precious library, and contemplates
works of art—neoclassical statues and expressionis-
tic paintings—which are often changed, just as there
are changes in the light effects and the fountains that
play in the garden, which is rich with noble flowers, yet perhaps somewhat severe; after all, he is a
prisoner. He does not know the name of the crime
for which he has been condemned, and can only be
amazed at the nature of his prison, from which he
cannot exit, but which is spacious, elegant, and only
slightly solitary. And, really, it is not absolutely final
that he has no way of leaving it: since the sovereign
has his whims. A door exists, and before all else he
has to find it. The residence has dozens of doors
that open onto walls. Dozens more open into empty
rooms that lead to nowhere; others into rooms which
lead, by way of another door, into rooms where still
a further door leads back to the room of the initial
door—the design of a brief labyrinth. Every door is
locked, and he has no keys; but there are also doors
which keys in any case do not open, and which in-

stead swing back only in response to verbal orders, pronounced aloud. These doors, too, have locks, but locks which are illusory. He has not been told if the door that leads to freedom is closed by key, or if instead it can be opened by the spoken word. If in fact it's a matter of the latter, he will have to find the formula that makes the door swing back. If he so desires, he'll be given an envelope containing a series of questions, and from the answers he will have to deduce the liberatory phrase. The questions change every day, and are apparently simple: Greek mythology, though not its most obvious points; the lives of the saints; the prisoner's childhood memories; numbers and their meanings; Latin palindromes in verse, to be translated without altering their form; cryptic anamorphoses; classical quotations. It's a game. The prisoner feels flattered, and is almost pleased that his freedom depends on the caprice of a cultivated prince. Were it not for the fact that inside its sumptuous dress his body is plagued by parasites, he would abandon his search for that door.

EIGHTY

*W*_{*hen*} *appointed custo-*
dian of the public toilets, he felt at first a certain
humiliation; and certainly his task was and remains
a humble one. He had to clean the tiles, mop up the
water, present the paper to those who asked for it,
open to demanding clients the stall that holds the
bidet. On the social scale of the society in which he
lives, he was and remains at a very low level, lower
even than the street sweeper who works in the open
air. He remains, in fact, in the toilets for many hours
every day and never sees the sun, since the toilets are
underground, and open from morning to evening.
His toilet is exclusively male, which pleases him,
since he is timid in character and would find it highly
embarrassing to open a booth for a lady. The environ-
ment in which he works is damp, always tepid, of a
temperature that doesn't much vary from one season
to the next; the facilities are not perfect, since water
is frequently missing, or one of the two wash basins
does not function, and those who have urinated form
a line to wash their hands, or return outside with
dirty hands, and this does not seem right to him.
He receives a salary, and those who descend into the
urinal generally leave him a small tip; all the same,
he had suffered for quite some time. Then, gradually, he started not to suffer, not because he no longer
feels the poverty of his work, but because of feeling
now that it is simply work. He has come, indeed, to

feel a certain pride. Holding so low a post on the social scale gives him a dignity, since the toilet attendants throughout the city are barely a dozen, and they constitute its lowest point, and thus an extreme; and not everyone is capable of reaching an extreme of anything. Now, moreover, another change is taking place within him; in fact, he has come to see that the man who urinates, the man who retreats into a hole to defecate, is radically different from the man who walks the city streets: he is a man who does not lie, who knows himself to be a creature, a transit of food-stuffs, and mortal; and at the very same time he sees in the man who urinates, leaning against the tiles, the man distracted by his own feces, by the sinister efficiency of his body, by the uncertainty of what it means that the human being employs its genitals for urination. This lowest of places is also a catacomb, and the toilet custodian realizes that the gesture of urination contains a supplication, is ugliness and reality, the lowest and the highest: he now considers his urinal a church, himself an officiant.

EIGHTY-ONE

In the city governed by the Bloody Princess, all the men fall sooner or later in love with her and present themselves at court to ask for her hand in marriage. She never says no, but poses a question to the man who asks for her hand in marriage: at times the question is complicated; at times it is simple, precisely like the questions asked in elementary schools. But no matter what the question is, the suitor will inevitably make an error, perhaps an irrelevant error, but an error which never escapes the Princess, and the suitor will be put to death. On the following day a new pretender will present himself, and will have no different a fate. In reality, the Princess is a tender and affectionate woman who would have no greater desire than to marry a fine young man who possesses neither title nor fortune, and to abandon her terrible task, since indeed it is nothing other than a task imposed upon her. The Princess, in fact, must obey a Bloody King, who supplies her with her questions, examines their solutions, indicates the inevitable error, and then, as well, imparts the order to proceed to the execution of the audacious suitor. But the Bloody King in turn curses his evil task and would hope for nothing better than to be able to read the classics, and to voyage in search of ancient cathedrals and books which men have forgotten. He would never wish the death of anyone, and not infrequently he sheds his tears along with his much loved Princess, but he must obey the Bloody Emperor. Every week the Emperor summons the King, and inquires as to how many men have been put to death, and in what way; and when the King describes the horrid fate of those cautionless young men, the Emperor nods in assent as he listens, as though everything were going precisely as he desired; and in closing he congratulates the King, who in his heart of hearts is tearing his hair and cursing both the Emperor and himself. In reality the Emperor is a hearty, corpulent fellow who loves the hunt, and good rich foods, wine, and bouts of after-dinner song; he plays with the dogs and cats, and makes a point of being generous to the poor; but he too must obey. Every month he leaves his castle and travels to a place in the high mountains, at the mouth of a cave which he dare not enter; but standing in place on the threshold, he recounts aloud the number of people put to death and where and how. From inside the cave a voice responds with growls and roars, and might even be the voice of a dragon, or of a volcano, or of a ghost. Strangely, that voice subsides into a kind of murmur, which has something kind about it. The Emperor then wraps his cape around himself and sets out again toward his castle, wondering who it may be he obeys, whether a demon or a god, and if what he obeys is itself a demon who obeys a god, or a god enslaved by the devil.

EIGHTY-TWO

*E*very now and then, let's say with a rhythm of two or three times a month, this gentleman gets telephone calls which perhaps are not intended for him, but which in any case leave him at times disturbed, at times embarrassed, at times excited, always saddened. Various voices irrupt into his fairly isolated existence and speak to him, distractedly, of images of life which he does not frequent. It's not at all rare for him to receive proposals for crimes, complicities in sordid gestures, frauds; he is confronted with offers for drugs, for women who are "guaranteed syphilitic," for the still warm corpses of famous ladies. He listens with horror, with cowardice, with excitement. His poor and uneventful life is enriched with a sinister extravagance, he feels himself to stand at the center of a powerful web of remarkable infamies, of endless impieties, of blasphemous apparitions. The voices that phone him change, but he suspects that he has been able to identify at least three of them. One is a male voice, adolescent, that gives him hasty appointments, he does not know if for small but audacious thefts, or for bolder corporeal understandings; the appointments are always imprecise, impossible to keep, but imparted with an imperative, impatient tone; sometimes they name the place, but not the time, and the place turns out to be non-existent; at times they insist on a moment that amounts to a provocation: "I'll meet you yesterday, in the central square." Another voice is female, and speaks to him only of carnal interchanges, of betrayals, of escapes, of complicities; at times this voice is full of suppli-cation and begs to be received, it wants to enter his life, but as soon as he is tempted to believe in this vocal hallucination, the woman upbraids him for his masculine insolence, his emotional stinginess, and behaves in every way like a woman unjustly spurned. At times she gives him appointments in non-existent houses, which he never attempts to reach. The third voice, male, elicits the image of a man who is very old. It might, the gentleman has said to himself, be the voice of someone dead and gone he once knew. The old man speaks monotonously of irrelevant and random things: the weather, the Boer war, the dances which once had been popular many many years, or even centuries, earlier. He never seems to expect a re-ply, and his talk is imprecise, like the talk of a person who moves among memories of which he has lost the order. In this voice, at times, the gentleman had the impression of catching some of the features of his own inflections.

EIGHTY-THREE

These two friends are linked by a singular complicity: the first believes that he's a sex maniac, the second believes himself afflicted by a homicidal mania. The situation, in itself far from dull, is further complicated by the fact that both consider themselves to be aesthetes, and as such are committed to the contemplation of their manias. The result is that the sex maniac displays a singular chastity, and the homicidal maniac an unnatural but elegant timidity. Each, in fact, has entrusted the other with the task of pursuing his own particular mania: so the sex maniac must satisfy the homicidal mania of his friend, and the homicidal maniac must live out the sexual mania of his comrade. Naturally enough, the homicidal maniac is entirely inept in the guise of a sexual offender, as his friend knows perfectly well. In the very same way, the sex manic would be incapable of carrying out the most modest and obvious of homicides. So, they have each decided to accept what the other pretends: the sex maniac asks the homicidal maniac to perform some savagery, and the homicidal maniac agrees; he returns within twenty-four hours and delivers a report, telling tales of rapes, orgies, humiliated girls: of course he has not done any of that, the very idea fills him with horror, and if ever he were to see a lady menaced by a brute, he would rush to her defense, like a knight of old. But in the name of the affection that ties him to his friend, he is willing to pretend to be an abject miscreant. In exchange, the sex maniac will on one of the following days minutiously describe to him a terrible and ingenious crime, carried out in such subtle and imaginative, in addition to improbable, circumstances, as to make it impossible for any newspaper to carry the slightest report of it, if not with years of delay. The homicidal maniac will thus live out a number of days in perfect bliss, giving alms to the poor, and donations to the parish, in thanks for having encountered so dear a friend. In reality, each knows that the other is entirely innocent, but also realizes that a friendship between two innocents would not accord with the abysses of their souls. They have therefore decided, secretly, that each of them will be the other's demon, since only in this way can they cultivate a delicate, responsive, attentive friendship.

EIGHTY-FOUR

He awakens in the middle of the night with the clear, sudden awareness of never having understood the Allegories of his own life. All of life is a fabric of Allegories, and now, in the dark, he attempts for the first time to decipher a few of them. There is first of all his wife, who sleeps beside him. Might she not be the Allegory of Justice? Of Discipline? He can't make it out, but he glances toward his wife, whose outline is barely visible, with a sense of caution, as though he lay beside something of enormous scope. Does one turn, perhaps, in the course of living, into a different Allegory? Could it be that his wife was once the Allegory of Life as Meaning, and now lives on as Order of the World? So, what's the panel in which one sees the severe and solemn figure of his wife? And where is the transfiguration of the Allegory of Meaning? His mind now turns to his two children: as a unit, they might constitute the Allegory of the Future; and, without their being aware of it, the Allegory of Meaning might thus have been passed on to them. But there are two of them, a boy and a girl. The boy could be the Allegory of Strength, the Constructor; but he doubts it; maybe he's the Allegory of Game. And his daughter? He thinks for an instant that perhaps she's the Allegory of Consoling Death. But it's possible too that his daughter doesn't belong to the particular system of allegories in which he lives, and is in some way preparing herself to belong to another system, where she'll start her allegorical career as Allegory of Meaning. He thinks with slight discomfort of the woman with whom he entertains a more or less clandestine relationship: is she the Allegory of Humility, or of Humiliation? He thinks back to other women, deposited in the memory of a joyless past, and thinks he recognizes Life as Malediction, the Obvious, Impossible Facility, Absence. He discovers, in the depths, the unforgotten Sickness of Birth. He thinks back to his father as the Allegory of Slowness, and to his mother as...as what? False Providence? Is there such a thing as that? And himself, himself awake in the middle of the night, what would he be, as an Allegory? Perhaps his wife, perhaps the other woman, could help him to interpret himself. On his own, he's unable to see himself, he can only touch his dying body. How does an Allegory die? He shakes his head; he lost all self-respect some time ago; he suspects that he's the Allegory of Incapability in Understanding Allegories.

EIGHTY-FIVE

Waking up. He always wakes up with a feeling of disorientation. His disorientation does not derive from any doubt about where he is, but from absolute certainty. He is in his house, where he has lived for many years. The fact of waking up in his house, in a place he already knows to be indifferent to him, is boring; it causes him a slight irritation, like a miniaturized desperation, fit to be applied to an insect. In the night he has made the acquaintance of something, and, no, it is not happiness, but a relationship with something central. He dreamed, and even though his dreams, thinking back to them now, seem devoid of meaning, in the moment in which he dreamed them they were central. So, from the point of view of himself awake, the center lies within the meaningless. He thinks back to his dreams, to the unforeseeable incidents, to the figures he sees appear and disappear in a lavish, impenetrable progress. The feeling returns that meaning lay in the hallucinated night, and that the world he re-enters each morning is true absence of meaning. Absence of meaning is coherent and foreseeable; meaning is enigmatic and aloof. Where one doesn't understand, one is close to the center of things; where one does, one stands at their furthest edge, outside of it. He would like to begin the day with a prayer; he does not know what or how to pray, but he does know his prayer's intent: to introduce into the day's coherence the incoherence of meaningful hallucination. Perhaps he might utter senseless words, or only emit sounds. But since he is awake, he cannot simulate being elsewhere, in the center of the world, where everything is image. His day begins with washing and evacuation; with his excrements, he expels the meanings which have entered his body during the night. Sometimes he wonders if hidden in his excrements there are not extraordinary images, if his feces are not desperation, or indecorous prayer. He smiles, without mirth. Now he must get up, and he does not know why; no matter what the day will bring him, he will always, essentially, be in waiting. In the morning he prepares himself for that fathomless moment of the day, that moment of peace and solitude, in which he awaits his entry into the night, his admission to the teeming home of deformed and indecipherable images of the center.

EIGHTY-SIX

He often wonders if the
problem of his relationship with the sphere is not
by its nature irresolvable. The sphere is not always
present before his eyes; all the same, when it goes
somewhere else, even when it retreats and hides, the
sphere is active, and he's aware that the universe
takes a certain form since it must host the sphere.
At times as he awakens in the half dark room—the
day has begun for everyone else, but he likes to get
up late, or, rather than late, he likes to get up tar-
dily—the sphere already hovers at the center of the
space; he examines it attentively, since the sphere demands attention, like a question. The sphere is not
always the same color, it shows gradations from gray
to black. At times, and these are the most disquieting
moments, the sphere turns inside out, and its place
is taken by a spherical cavity, an entirely lightless
emptiness. At times, the sphere will remain absent
for several days; rarely, however, for more than ten.
It suddenly reappears at any hour at all, for no com-
prehensible reason, as though returning from a trip,
from a slightly culpable but agreed-upon absence.
He has the impression that the sphere pretends to
beg his pardon, while in reality being ironic, and,
even though with innocence, malign. To cancel that
repulsive presence from his life, he had attempted
on one occasion the use of violence; but the sphere
is reserved and elusive, except when it itself decides

to strike; and then in whatever point of the body it touches, it generates an opaque, desolate, lacerating pain. However, the sphere's most typical act of hostility lies in interposing itself between him and something he is trying to see. The sphere in such cases is capable of assuming minute dimensions, a restless little ball that scuds before his eyes. He still remains tempted to confront the sphere with sudden brutality, nearly as though he did not know it to be made of nothing one might strike; or he contemplates taking flight, and re-beginning a life in a place unknown to the sphere. But he does not believe such a thing to be possible; he thinks he must persuade the sphere not to exist, and he knows this slow seduction into nothingness to follow the ins and outs of a slow and labyrinthine path, patient and minutiously astute.

EIGHTY-SEVEN

*O*ne *clearly sees that man*
to be uneasy. He is restless; he walks, he halts, he
stands on a single foot, he takes off again at a run.
He peeks warily around the corner of the next street;
he sighs, and leans against the wall. He is in fact extremely disgruntled with his life, but his notions concerning the origins of such disgruntlement are highly confused. It might, he thought, be a question of
the use of time. Time follows no rules, yet pretends
to. Nothing is more difficult than dealing with time.
There are days when the seconds rush by as though
having escaped from an hourglass set up for use as
a prison; but often they are of various sizes, and in
living his life he constantly stumbles over them. He
thinks he still has many years to live, but he does
not know how long they will be. He fiddles with the
mental buttons of time, and suddenly it stands completely still. From one hour to the next, ten hours
pass; the seconds are as long as streets, and streets,
we know, are always made of quarters of an hour,
but four streets don't make an hour, they make six
days. The seventh is a square, and however you cross
it is always a mistake. He has attempted to tame the
future, and to force it into a less fatiguing rhythm.
He has purchased a great clock, to teach time time,
but time refuses to learn itself. If he pushes another button, time flies, takes off, flees. The streets
shorten, and if he doesn't immediately brake, his

life will be over within a week, and he will have done nothing to justify his birth. Someone ought to invent a clock capable of capturing time, of forcing it to hold the same pace, always, every day, his whole life long. But he himself would be the first to break such a clock to pieces. So, he can only seek out provisional agreements, provisional and treacherous, since time doesn't stick to agreements, not because it's deceitful, but because it is itself in turn the victim of time. In reality, as the discontented gentleman has suspected for quite some time, time too is discontented with itself, and has no way to resolve its uneasiness, since it has no gauge, other than itself, with which to measure itself. The result, of course, is uselessly correct, and time never knows if it is running, if it is dawdling, if it is standing still. So, time is always begging everybody's pardon, while not even knowing if there's any reason to do so.

EIGHTY-EIGHT

In the half-abandoned city, devastated by the plague and by history, there live only a few persons, who continually move from one house to another. The city's dismal history has left the survivors, and the few who rushed to join them, inclined to an abstract and meditative attitude. Since the houses are innumerable, if somewhat dilapidated, everyone searches out a home that's congenial to the mood, the studies, the trials of the moment. A gray-haired gentleman, once the cook of a now defunct king, likes to live in a five-storey building, with thirty rooms on each floor. When interested in history, he lives on the first floor, on the second he meditates on Providence, on the third he reconstructs and inter-prets his dreams and his past, to the fourth he en-trusts metaphysics, and asceticism to the fifth. There are five bedrooms on each floor, which he uses ac-cording to whether he is gloomy, sulky, melancholy, irritated, or indifferent; it is not foreseen that he be cheerful, but if he were, he would sleep on the floor. A minute and restless gentleman seeks out cottages and bungalows, with small rooms that he makes even smaller by constructing partitions; he's an aficionado of moans, of murmurs, of sighs, and in small spaces he hears them better; he is making notes for a great work on sighs; to be sure of never ceasing to sigh, he attentively cultivates an unhappiness as minuscule as he is. The mayor of the city—which in reality has no mayor, but one of its inhabitants is called "the mayor" without his being aware of it—has three houses: a column with a winding staircase and a room at its top; a catacomb with Latin inscriptions; a lion's cage: he sees them as corresponding to the three moments of the Spirit, the Unconscious Shades, and the Instincts. When the wind is impetuous, one hears here and there a great collapsing sound: some house succumbs to time, and a rain is enough to turn it into a heap of mud that blocks the street. An obstinate gentleman, who at one time played the basset-horn in a classical orchestra, collects wall fragments, bricks, stones, and intends in the middle of an abandoned park to construct a labyrinth, which at its center will have a one-room house; he has drawn up the plan of the labyrinth, and on finishing its construction, he will burn that document. His behavior is generally held to be not very sociable.

EIGHTY-NINE

*A*t the beginning, when
they first met, they loved each other because both of
them, in different ways, had known an extreme and
lonely unhappiness. Her life had been profoundly
bitter, his precociously unfortunate. They conjoined
their bitterness and misfortune, and lovingly attempted to help one another, they succeeded in help-
ing one another, while experiencing neither a cessa-
tion of her bitterness nor a metamorphosis of his
misfortune. With the strength of their tie's unique-
ness, of the negativity that distinguished it, they
built up around their sadness a constant, faithful,
attentive love. They consoled each other while being
fully aware that no consolation was possible. Each
continued to be what she or he had been in their
previous lives, and together they lived a relationship
that did not deny but in some way made common
property of their pain. But love has its ruses. For a
while, love passed reciprocally across the bitterness
or misfortune that marked the condition of him or
her, the one and the other; but since that condition
was the basis and the guarantee and the meaning of
their love, each began to love directly the bitterness
or misfortune of the other; each took on the task of
being the custodian of the other's condition, and
began to grow cautious that the other should not
too much depart from that condition's pains. Each
became jealous of the pain of the other, and in short

would have seen an act of infidelity in any attempt on the part of the other to abandon that pain. Since by nature both of them were constant, each learned to love his or her own pain as a pledge to the love of the other; so each protected his or her own pain and kept vigil over the pain of the other. Their love thus reached a perfect equilibrium in which each attained the other's center, by traversing and controlling the territory of the other's anguish. Every day, each checked that his or her own and the other's anguish were intact. They tried, indeed, to increase and perfect their sufferings; each at first by increasing his or her own; later, by working to increase the other's. They plumbed each other to the depths, and with patience and discernment they reciprocally transfixed each other, and allowed themselves to be transfixed. Each accompanied the other toward an irreversible degradation. Now, not unaware of it, they are attentively preparing their meticulous, slow, reciprocal destruction.

NINETY

The city is extremely poor. Its citizens quite some time ago abandoned all attempts to modify their condition, and live a solitary, excluded, taciturn existence. Slowly, the population diminishes, though not because anyone emigrates— no one has the imagination to go off "to make their fortune," as the saying goes—but because the dead are not replaced; if a child is born, which is very rare, it is offered to the neighboring cities, where someone will be found to adopt it. The houses are old and constructed of materials which already reveal the signs of a continuous, by now precipitous decline. There is no true and proper work, but every so often a certain number of citizens are ordered to transport a few stones—three, five—from one street to the next. If there are five stones, ten citizens come, and each does half the trip; they are paid with worn, illegible coins which are not legal tender in any city. They frequently lose them, since in the city there is nothing to buy. They live on the stingy produce of gardens cultivated by people who know nothing about and do not love the cultivation of gardens. Since they have these gardens, they never, or almost never, go out into the streets. They have the impression it's about to rain, no matter what the weather. There are no tailors, and their clothes slowly waste away, but since their uses are minimal, they will be able to last until the city's total extinction. The origins of so much poverty are unknown. Perhaps it can be attributed to disorderly religious crises, which resulted in a lethal disorientation. Or to a network of simultaneous disappointments in love, which set men and women apart from one another, pushing some into spinster- and bachelorhood, others into marriages without desire and without love. For many years, at this point, no one in this city has fallen in love, and even though they read love stories in the long empty hours, it's all considered a deceitful game. Study commissions came at first to visit the city, in order to grasp the mechanism of this incredible poverty. A circus was invited to come to the city, and for two days, free of charge, gave shows in the central square. Only one man attended: a deaf man who had the impression he was going to a religious funeral service. The rest of the city's inhabitants remained locked up in their homes, all intensely pained by that luxurious din. It can't be said that they were waiting for their own and their city's final demise; they obscurely knew that they were that demise.

NINETY-ONE

In his previous incarnation,
that man was a horse. This is something of which he
is fully aware, in light of unassailable evidence: his
favorite shoes, his food, the way he laughs. All the
same, for a great deal of time he was not alarmed:
he knows, in fact, that such conditions are not rare,
but often do not endure. A noctambulous friend of
his, formerly an owl, turned diurnal in his thirties,
and now has a family; and a rattlesnake is now a
subtle—only slightly venomous, in memory of her
former state—art critic. He noted, however, proceeding through the years, that his symptoms tended less
to disappear than to grow more complicated. This
led him to begin to experience a certain anxiety, and
fear as well, especially when he felt impelled to skit-
tishness, or to take to flight, or to rearing up, in the
grip of a will which remained obscure to him. He did
not know, in fact, that he had inhabited not a single
incarnation as a horse, but three consecutive ones:
first he had been a horse as thin as a shadow, jaded,
depressed and inept, and soon to waste away in dole-
ful, slovenly patience; then a massive draft horse,
good at pulling wagons, stout and humble; and finally he had passed through a small agile race horse,
more ambitious than intelligent, and a wrangler and
a troublemaker who would halt to set misunderstandings straight in the middle of a race. In general
terms, none of the three had had the stuff to cancel

out a lingering air of frustration, nearly as though all three had been involved in an identical defeat, abasement, precocious consumption. That man who felt within himself the remnant of a horseness continued at length to reflect on a single horse; and only bit by bit did he begin to suspect that his bizarre and incongruous reactions came from several horses. From that moment on, he began to make the effort first of all to establish contact with and then to untangle the horses of his past. He recognized the race horse, but attributing to the race horse the potency of the draft horse, he supposed it to have been a great trotter; so he finds it hard to understand whether, in addition to the racer, there are two, or one, or several horses. Meanwhile, his symptoms do not disappear, indeed they grow more perverse; and they leave him debilitated. The more he probes within himself, the more he seems to discover horses: galloping horses, horses beneath the rain, horses at the slaughterhouse, horses gone crazy, beaten horses, horses tamed by an unknown, pitiless hand. He rants, frenzies, rages, cries, and when at times he whinnies, he halts and attempts to understand which of so many horses —suspected by now to be a herd—has whinnied through his human mouth.

NINETY-TWO

O_n *reaching a certain*
point of the road, one has to be aware that, hidden
in the gullies and brush, there may be bandits. The
bandits are small, haggard, malnourished, and sad;
they have no firearms, but only pieces of wood cut
into the shapes of rifles, and in an utterly infantile
way. Only an accomplice could pretend to fear their
turning into roadside assassins; all the same, the
adventure of encountering the bandits carries so ro-
mantic an air that very few of the area's inhabitants
are willing to do without it, especially in the seasons
of fine weather. People go out in carriages, since the
ambush comes off better with a carriage than in a car
or on the train. Generally, whole families travel together, along with the children and the servants. For
the children, the attack of the highwaymen is a kind
of initiation ceremony, and those who have been assaulted have stories to tell up until their wedding day.
No one in this city, in fact, goes any longer to the theater or the circus: they all remain at home and talk
about the bandits, especially those who have been
attacked to those who haven't been. When a comfortable bourgeois family goes out to have itself attacked,
a reasonable quantity of money is taken along—not
an ostentatious amount, but not cheapskatish—as
well as a few knick-knacks: beginning with those
gifts that circulate from one wedding to the next, and
nobody knows where to put. When they arrive at one

of the ambush places, they make a show of speeding up, of keeping a sharp lookout, since they think the bandits find this comforting, and the bourgeois families see their gesture as socially responsible and laudable. For some time now, however, the bandits have grown more rare; assaults have diminished, and there has also been an inquiry into the nature of what may have happened. It seems that a number of bandits have moved on to holding ambushes on the outskirts of a neighboring city, where people who go out to be assaulted don't bring along old wedding presents. Thanks, in fact, to a Story of Art published in installments, the bandits have recently developed a sense of taste, and realized that the homes in which they lived, full of alabaster greyhounds and life-size dolls, were ugly. This has brought about a tension between the two cities, which had never looked favorably toward one another. Currently, the city that suffers ever fewer lootings—a month has gone by since the last—is debating whether to declare itself to have routed the bandits, or to try to attract them back with more interesting spoils: drawings by well-known artists, leather-bound books, antique chests.

NINETY-THREE

The inventor of the black swan is a melancholy man who seldom removes his coat, and who desires to live in a possibly kinder universe; this is why he has committed himself to the swan—an elegant, taciturn animal that moves on the surface of lakes—and in addition has given it the fascination of a putative widowhood. He considers the black swan to be one of his happiest inventions, and the black swan rewards him by regarding him from afar with eyes overflowing with affectionate melancholy. On foggy mornings, the melancholy gentleman comes to the shore of the lake and waits in tender anxiety for the re-appearance of the only black swan in existence. Since it is unique, it is not, properly speaking, widowed; but precisely this is the subtlety: it is a matter of intrinsic widowhood, of a "loss-of-the-nonexistent," and thus of a thing that cannot be repaired by any intrigue of the heart, which are things specifically denied to the swan, which is black. He is uncertain as to whether or not to create a second black swan, and thus to form a pair. He mentally admires the pair of silent, regal swans, but fears that a pair might in some way diminish the integrity of that sad black. He might create another black swan, but not set it out in the same tract of water, but in some distant and inaccessible place— since his swans would have brief flight, and clipped wing. All the same, each swan should have some sort of notion of the existence, somewhere else, on other waters, of a similar swan, and of itself and the other as the only ones to wear that color; in such a circumstance, their sadness would not be entrusted only to a solitary languor, but would sharpen—incurable sore—by way of their awareness of the existence, invisible and unreachable, of a being with which to converse. He alone would know where the two swans are found, and this private knowledge would make him not only a creator, which he already is, but a creator who contributes to his creations' unhappiness, and thus an ambiguous, binary being, who alternates and intermixes enmity and love. Insofar as he alternates, he is terrible and extremely sweet; insofar as he intermixes, he is himself the depository of the world's unhappiness, of the sadness of which the two black swans, as they glide, reciprocally known and unknown to each other, over distant and silent waters, are no more than a poignant example.

NINETY-FOUR

He turned the corner, cer-
tain that it would be there, waiting for him, and ready
perhaps to greet him with a smile. He found nothing,
and now we see him as he runs the length of the great
street, passes the bolted gates—he wants to reach the
square before it does. But the square is empty. So, approach from the front is useless, the same as pursuit.
Perhaps it likes to pursue. He now walks slowly, with
unnatural slowness. Every now and then he halts, as
though to examine things which don't exist. He discovers gifts of patience, but also a certain inclination
to fear. He brusquely spins around, there is nothing
behind him, but he feels all the same that something
has disappeared, that a being has brusquely decided
its withdrawal from existence. He fixes his eyes on
the emptiness, as though to make it understood that
he is looking at the place which was occupied by what
he hoped to meet. He returns to walking, now with
studied, haughty, insolent indifference. He does not
know if it takes offense at injurious treatment, but
surely he is certain of desiring to offend it. He would
like to be struck, assaulted, bitten; he would like to
be captured and abused by an enemy. Since nothing
happens, he quickens his pace again, and runs; and
while running he squirms and gesticulates, pretending to be attacked by something viscid and ferocious,
but alive; he screams, cries, shuns, cuts across the
street, in order to seem a prey, even an easy prey,

and the object of implacable pursuit. He thinks of himself as a deer, as a boar, as a buck. He bites his hands until drawing blood, since he knows that the odor of blood incites pursuers; he dirties a kerchief with blood and throws it behind him, to leave a trace. On reaching a cross-roads, he stops, he crouches down, he covers his head and face with his hands as though to defend himself from an imminent, pitiless aggression. The silence remains intact. He lies down as though he had fainted or were dead, since some are fond of exhausted prey, even cadavers. He stands back up, and once again begins pursuit, as though pressing forward to face what at that very moment was following on his heels. The two perhaps traverse each other, remaining unaware of it. He halts. He is exhausted. He looks above, at the window sills, he walks through the flower beds, he gathers flowers, knowing that the odor of flowers can also be a lure. He urinates on his hands so as to give off a scent of wildness, of meat to be brought down. Nothing happens. Nothing has ever happened. He regains composure, washes, throw away the flowers. He'll try again tomorrow, with a different moon, along different streets.

NINETY-FIVE

With extreme amazement,
he noted, at the bus stop, a snow white unicorn. He
was greatly surprised, because the unicorn had occupied a whole chapter in his treatise on the Things
that do not exist; at the time he had been very well-
versed in the field of Things that do not exist, and
had received excellent grades; his professor, indeed,
had counseled him to specialize in the Things that
do not exist. It's clear, of course, that the study of
the Things that do not exist includes the clarification
of the reasons for which they cannot exist, and of
the ways in which they don't exist, since the Things
can be impossible, self-contradictory, incompatible,
extra-spatio-temporal, anti-historical, recessive, im-
plosive, or not exist in many other ways as well. The
unicorn was absolutely anti-historical, and yet here's
one now, at the bus stop, and the people standing
around don't seem to take any notice. But extraordinary happenings weren't yet over: the unicorn, in
fact, was chatting—no other word would do—with a
figure that remained out of sight; then a bus arrived,
and the unicorn gave a parting greeting to this figure
who was out of sight and boarded the bus, "display-
ing," as the saying goes, a season ticket. And there,
now in sight, one saw a basilisk, of medium stature,
with very thick dark glasses. Now, the basilisk is a
complicated animal, and its non-existence is attributed to "excess." It is also an animal described as

dangerous—its eyes have "impossible" powers—and this, he found himself thinking, was why the basilisk was wearing glasses. The basilisk had a satchel under one arm, and when a bus approached, he opened it and pulled something out of it—wasn't that a Medusa's head?—something that looked at the bus number and reported it back to him, since it was clear that with wearing such glasses he couldn't see anything on his own. The specialist in Things that do not exist was greatly disturbed. Was he maybe going crazy? He didn't think so. He set to wandering about with no clear goal and met a tragelaph, a phoenix, and an amphisbaena on a bicycle; a satyr asked for directions to via Macedonio Melloni, and a gentleman bearing his head in the middle of his chest asked him the time and politely thanked him for the information. On beginning to see the fairies, the elves and the guardian angels, he had the feeling of having always lived in a city deserted of human beings, or populated by extras; then he began to ask himself if the World too, the World itself, is a Thing that does not exist.

NINETY-SIX

A man with an insatiable
appetite for dreams dreamed so much that in the
building where he lived no one else was able to
dream, except perhaps when the dreamer went to
the sea or the mountains on vacation. An irritating
and impossible situation, and the building's tenants,
all of them people of fine background—professors,
dukes, proprietors of construction companies, and
an international hit man—made their objections
heard. The gentleman's response was not well-
mannered, and the question began to rankle. No one
in the building dreamed anymore, and—because
that gentleman dreamed entirely in full color, and
undertook experiments in three-dimensionality—
even the people in the neighboring condominiums
dreamed little, and in small format, and in black
and white. The dispute ended up in court, where it
was determined that the gentleman was involved in
illegal use of the dreams of others, and had to put
an end to it, since he was falling short of the norms
of good-neighborly behavior. But of course it is not
easy to persuade someone to restore possession of
dreams, or not to appropriate dreams which do not
belong to him. The gentleman continued to dream
all the dreams in the building, and only the international hit man managed, every now and then, to
dream a small, stupid dream.

But the greedy dreamer realized before too

long that something had changed; since he dreamed the dreams of all his co-tenants, and since his co-tenants were annoyed with him, and if given the chance would have dreamed dreams in which he was a negative figure, he began to have dreams in which, in addition to himself, there was also another himself, despicable and brutal. He attempted to throw him out of his dreams, but couldn't. And slowly he began to suffer from dream disturbances, to be restless, and to feel no self-esteem. His dreams were full of quarrels, and he often woke up breathless, with a sense of persecution, psychologically shattered. He fell ill. He wasted away. He grew depressed. Finally, he decided to dream less, and first of all not to dream his neighbors' dreams. He in fact had felt unsafe in one of the duke's dreams, and awoke in a cold sweat from a dream that belonged to the hit man. All of the building's residents have now returned to dreaming. Friendly gestures have been made toward the greedy dreamer, but he is too depressed to respond to them. His own dreams are not enough for him. And now, at times, he's seen to walk through squalid and disreputable neighborhoods, and he attempts to steal dreams from lower-class, uncultivated people; they are not first-rate dreams, but by now he is addicted to dreams, and will make himself a thief, a bandit, in order every night to have all those dreams—even if not his own, even if ugly and senseless—which, monstrous horde, are wearing him down, and leading him to catastrophe.

NINETY-SEVEN

Gentlemen: we must ask you please to follow and pay close attention to the itinerary. The place is still inactive, but there can nonetheless be dangers. The portal is low, so watch your wings. Here now, let's stop for a moment; you can rest against the handrail. You'll note the vastness of this place, which all the same is only the first compartment. It would take a human being years to cross it. A lifetime would not be enough. Up there, on the left, you'll see a series of cells. They are closed by gates of inconsumable iron, because the sufferings of those who abide there must be observed by the guards. As need be, the cells can be red hot or frozen. The gates are walled into place, and have no locks. Lower down, you see those rectangles, like stone plaques; they lead down into a cell in the shape of a tomb, but its floor is purest fire. They are easy to open from the outside, only once, impossible from the inside; a peep-hole permits a view of what takes place within. Now, come this way, to the left. On the wall before you, you see those enormous vents: they spew out darkness. No matter how impossible it may seem, the darkness can be indefinitely increased. Whoever is involved in the darkness will see it grow uninterruptedly, eternally. Please follow us. We are entering a corridor: you'll note the spiked presses, the chains to be fired to a heat. If you clap your hands, you'll hear how deep the echo is; the dimensions here are enormous. For as far ahead as you can see, there are mobile lances that can thrust across the passageway from one side to the other. Here will be found a depot of replacement eyes, to be restored to those who must continually be blinded. Be careful here, step back: that's the mouth of a pit with perfectly smooth and vertical walls, and which all the same must be traveled by foot, always falling and never falling: practically, it has no bottom. This is the hall of the knives; the knives of course move on their own. This grappling-iron is used for reversals, where the body is turned inside out: the guts replace the skin, the head, the limbs. These gloves are made of worms that eat anything and everything, and they excrete in such a manner that what has been devoured is recomposed. At present the worms are inactive. This is the place of blood and urine. Gentlemen: I see that the hour is growing late; and this place, moreover, is endless. It will take some time to learn to move about in it, and above all to use it. I would like to ask you to be ready, tomorrow, an hour earlier than usual. Tomorrow is the day of the Creation of the World.

NINETY-EIGHT

*A*t *first, that sudden, quiet*
question brought a faint smile to his lips; but he
knew that his bizarrely thoughtful brain had at various times entangled him in fabular questions, fairy-
tale replies, mythological inquests. He was neither
theologian nor philosopher, and he did not know,
in spite of often having asked himself, whether in
fact he belonged to a religion, and if so to which.
He preferred the status of itinerant believer. Later
the problem returned to his mind, with a sudden,
imperative and sinister sound. And he stopped,
absent-mindedly, but not without apprehension, to
consider it. This was the problem: whether there is
a difference, and if so of what kind, between a person who has been dead five minutes, a person who
has been dead five years, two thousand years, five
hundred thousand years. If to die means to enter
into nothingness, dying now or having been dead for
half a million years would appear to make no difference. But is that really so? Nothingness is non-being,
but it need not be taken for granted that non-being
excludes time. If I can hypothesize a nothingness before my birth and a nothingness after my death, that
invites me to suspect that nothingness is not indifferent to the scansion of time, since surely the nothingness prior to birth is not—at very least as a question
of temporality—the nothingness of after death.
So, there is no nothingness as nothingness, without

extension in time, and the dead must be collocated in various temporal segments of nothingness. So the dead of half a million years ago are in a nothingness which is temporally extraneous to the nothingness of the recent dead, but not discontinuous with it. But he also knew that some suppose the dead to doze in insensate sleep, waiting for judgment day. So, does the sleep of departed souls preserve them, or is there a manner in which they age? Or, if they do not age, do they dream? One dream each century would be enough to cause a soul to age; so the dead man's soul of half a million years ago would be something on the order of a white-haired soul, perhaps the king of the dead. But one may as well suppose the more incredible and better established image that death coincides with a revelation, a discovery: and in such a case it's inevitable for the recent dead to be younger, and more inexpert, than those even only slightly longer dead. He asks if such a minimal difference can ever be assuaged, even in the course of a sojourn that endures forever. He is also disquieted by that nameless soul, that first and tentative project for a soul, of half a million years ago, a million years ago. So, hadn't there been a "first" to enter whatever we want to call it—be it nothingness, or light, or eternity? Or hadn't there been some empty eternity into which there entered a first disheveled and disoriented man who had no idea of what he was undergoing, and who first discovered the beyond? And is now this soul the oldest and most ancient of the dead, whom every other must salute? And will not he too have the obligation to salute him, as the only soul among the dead who knows the whole of the dead's experience?

NINETY-NINE

The young man stretches out on his bed, and patiently, cautiously attempts to find a position which he defines as the "position of surrender." First of all, he must ascertain if that position is allowed to him; and to do so he must investigate the way his legs, arms, belly, and even his fingers, hair, fingernails and eyes, relate to the whole world. Every time he makes this affirmation, it strikes him as demented and maniacal, yet all the same he remains unable to describe his search in any other terms. Moreover, there can be no doubt that at the moment in which he embarks on his investigation, he performs a mental gesture of abstraction from the world, and therefore, if only by virtue of a simple dialectic game, that he is not the world. At that point, whatsoever comes into contact with him is the starting point of the world, and the whole of the world, without hiatus, begins at the point of contact between his body and the world. Sometimes, indeed quite often, his body and the world are not at peace with one another: his legs apprehend the world as a harsh and persecutory sheath, his arms drown in the world, the world holds tight his fingernails, so they cannot scratch it. Then he knows that the position of peace has been denied to him; he does not attempt to find it, but somehow settles himself where he is, continuing to be at war, closes his eyes, and tends not so much toward sleep as to unconsciousness, which he considers a tool of war with respect to the world. There are times when the world restrains itself; it does not touch his body, and seems ignorant of his will to be the beginning of the world. So, he attempts in such cases to seduce it, and to inform it that, no, he is not at peace with it, but has surrendered to the world's totality, to all its modes of being. He curls up on the edge of his bed, bending his legs in such a way as to leave them slightly sticking out, to signify that he makes no attempt to defend himself, and proposes instead to enter the world, to situate his body in such a way that, no, he is no longer the world's beginning, but simply a place within it. If this gesture is accepted, he unfolds his arms and inspects all the parts of his body, with eyes closed. If none of its parts are fugitive or rebellious or exhibit desperation, or reveal signs of persecution, he then begs his body to disband, to dissolve its bonds with itself, and allow what's specific to his fingernails to pass along to his belly, and that his eyes have commerce with his big toe. For this to occur, the world must have taken possession of his body, and he thus will have found the rare and exquisite moment of surrender; and he finally will be able to accept, and, having laid aside the daggers of his daily life, to sleep.

ONE HUNDRED

A *writer is writing a book*
about a writer who is writing two books about two
writers, one of whom writes because he loves the
truth, and the other because it makes no difference
to him. These two writers write a total of twenty-two
books that talk about twenty-two writers, some of
whom lie without knowing they are lying, others lie
and know so, others seek the truth while knowing
they won't be able to find it, others believe themselves
to have found it, still others believed themselves to
have found it but have started to have doubts. The
twenty-two writers produce a total of three hundred
and forty-four books that talk about five hundred
and nine writers, since in more than one book a
writer marries a woman writer and they have from
three to six children who are all writers, except for
one who works in a bank and is killed in a robbery,
and then it's discovered that at home he was writing
a beautiful novel about a writer who goes to the bank
and is killed in a robbery; the robber, in reality, is the
son of the writer who's the protagonist of another
novel, and he had moved from one novel to another
because he found it simply intolerable to continue to
live alongside his father, who's the author of novels
on the decadence of the bourgeoisie, and in particular has written a family saga in which there is also a
young descendent of a novelist who has authored a
saga on the decadence of the bourgeoisie, and this

descendent runs away from home and becomes a robber who then in the course of a bank robbery kills not only a banker but also his own brother who had gotten into the wrong novel and was trying to pull some strings to get transferred to another. These five hundred and nine writers write eight thousand and two novels, in which there are twelve thousand writers, in round numbers, who write eighty-six thousand volumes in which there is only a single writer, a depressed and maniacal stutterer, who writes a single book about a writer who's writing a book about a writer, but decides not to finish it, and arranges an appointment with him and kills him, setting off a reaction that results in the death of the twelve thousand, the five hundred and nine, the twenty-two, the two, and the single initial author, who has thus achieved the goal of discovering, thanks to his intermediaries, the only necessary writer, whose end is the end of all the writers, including himself, the writer who is the author of all the writers.

A Note on the Author

GIORGIO MANGANELLI was born in Milan in 1922, but lived most of his adult life in Rome, where he died in 1990. After taking a degree in political science, conferred in 1942 by the University of Pavia, with a doctoral thesis on "the political doctrines of the seventeenth century" and prospects of entering the diplomatic corps, he in fact undertook a career (later abandoned) as an English professor at the University of Rome. In the early 1960s, he was a member of the avant-garde literary group "Gruppo '63," for which his *La letteratura come menzogna (Literature as Lie)* became a fundamental reference point. After the appearance of the Rizzoli edition of *Hilarotragoedia* in 1964 (reissued by Adelphi in 1987), he went on to publish a remarkable series of books in a highly original mixture of genres—novels, essays, commentaries, anatomies, *minima moralia*, travel books, and short stories, in addition to becoming known to a wider and more general public as a prolific reviewer and commentator in newspapers and magazines, and for television reportages. *Centuria* was first published in 1979 and was winner of that year's Viareggio Prize, which is generally held to be Italy's most prestigious literary award. Aside from the English translation of *Tutti gli errori (All the Errors,* McPherson & Co., 1990), Giorgio Manganelli's works have also appeared in French, German, Spanish, Dutch, Danish, Greek, Polish, Bohemian, Serbo-Croatian, and Hungarian.

PRINCIPAL WORKS

Hilarotragoedia (1964)

La letteratura come menzogna (1967)

GIORGIO MANGANELLI

Nuovo commento (1969)
Agli dèi ulteriori (1972)
Lunario dell'orfano sannita (1973)
Cina e altri orienti (1974)
A e B (1975)
Sconclusione (1976)
Cassia governa a Cipro (1977)
Pinocchio: un libro parallelo (1977)
Centuria (1979)
Amore (1981)
Angosce di stile (1981)
Discorso sull'ombra e dello stemma (1982)
Dall'inferno (1985)
Tutti gli errori (1986)
Rumori o voci (1987)
Antologia privata (1989)
Encomio del tiranno (1990)
La palude definitiva (1991)
Esperimento con l'India (1992)
Il presepio (1992)
Il rumore sottile della prosa (1994)
La notte (1996)
Le interviste impossibili (1997)
Il delitto rende ma è difficile (1997)
Salons (2000)
Improvvisi per macchina da scrivere (2003)

A Note on the Translator

HENRY MARTIN was born in Philadelphia, Pennsylvania, in 1942. He received a B.A. in English Literature from Bowdoin College in 1963 and an M.A. in English Literature from New York University in 1964. He has resided in Italy since 1965, where he works as a free-lance art critic, curator and translator. He has received translation grants from the New York State Council on the Arts and the National Endowment for the Arts, as well as a Critic's Fellowship from the National Endowment for the Arts. He is also the principal consultant for McPherson & Co.'s modern Italian fiction series. He is married to the artist Berty Skuber, and they live with their son John-Daniel in Southern Tyrol. Henry Martin's books include:

AS AUTHOR

Arman (New York: Harry Abrams, 1972)

An Introduction to George Brecht's 'Book of the Tumbler on Fire' (Milan: Edizioni Multhipla, 1978)

Part One: Never change anything. Let changes fall in. Einfallen. Es fällt mir ein. Part Two: Never say never. A conversation with George Brecht. (Lugo: Exit, 1979)

FAVORISCA: On the Work of Gianfranco Baruchello (Mantua: Casa del Mantegna, and Livorno: Museo Progressivo di Arte Contemporanea, 1982)

One Hundred Skies for Geoffrey Hendricks (Barkenhoff Foundation: Worpswede, 1986 and New York and Aica di Fiè: Money for Food Press, 1993)

Concerning George Brecht's VOID (Verona: Archive Conz, 2000)

AS CO-AUTHOR WITH GIANFRANCO BARUCHELLO
How to Imagine (Kingston, N. Y.: McPherson, 1983)
Why Duchamp (Kingston, N. Y.: McPherson, 1985)
Fragments of a Possible Apocalypse
(Milan: Edizioni Multhipla, 1978)

AS TRANSLATOR FROM GERMAN
The Passionate Gardener by Rudolf Borchardt
(Kingston, N. Y.: McPherson, 2005)

AS TRANSLATOR FROM ITALIAN
All the Errors, by Giorgio Manganelli
(Kingston, N. Y.: McPherson, 1990)
The Iguana, by Anna Maria Ortese
(Kingston, N. Y.: McPherson, 1987)
A Music Behind the Wall,
selected short stories by Anna Maria Ortese, 2 vols.
(Kingston, N. Y.: McPherson, 1994 & 1998)
The Father, by Luigi Zoja (London: Routledge, 2001)
Abortion: Loss and Renewal in the Search for Identity,
by Eva Pattis (London: Routledge, 1997)
Growth and Guilt, by Luigi Zoja
(London: Routledge, 1994)

AS TRANSLATOR FROM FRENCH AND GERMAN
Daniel Spoerri from A to Z
(Milan: Fondazione Mudima, 1991)